THE WALL OF THE SKY, THE WALL OF THE EYE

The Wall of the Sky, The Wall of the Eye

Stories by

JONATHAN LETHEM

faber and faber

First published in the United States in 1996
by Harcourt Brace & Company

This edition first published in the United Kingdom in 2002
by Faber and Faber Limited
3 Queen Square London WC1N 3AU

Photoset by RefineCatch Ltd., Bungay, Suffolk
Printed in England by Mackays of Chatham plc, Chatham, Kent

"The Happy Man" appeared, in slightly different form, in *Asimov's Science Fiction*. "Access Fantasy" appeared in *Starlight 2*. "Light and the Sufferer" appeared, in slightly different form, in *Century*. "How We Got in Town and out Again" appeared in *Asimov's Science Fiction*. "The Hardened Criminals" appeared, in slightly different form, in *Intersections: The Sycamore Hill Anthology*.

A CIP record for this book
is available from the British Library

ISBN 0–571–20599–2

2 4 6 8 10 9 7 5 3 1

Without Whom

Michael Kandel, Richard Parks, Gardner Dozois,
the Sycamore Hill Writers' Conference 1992 and 1994, and
Charles Rosen and Christian K. Messenger,
inspirers of *Dunk*.

The book's title is taken from a description of
Fritz Lang's films in Geoffrey O'Brien's
*The Phantom Empire: Movies in the Mind of
the Twentieth Century*.

"The Happy Man" *is for Stanley Ellin*
—otherwise, for Blake Lethem

Contents

The Happy Man 1
Access Fantasy 55
Light and the Sufferer 75
How We Got in Town and out Again 117
Five Fucks 148
The Hardened Criminals 172
Sleepy People 211

The Happy Man

1

I left her in the bedroom, and went and poured myself a drink. I felt it now; there wasn't any doubt. But I didn't want to tell her, not yet. I wanted to stretch it out for as long as I could. It had been so quick, this time.

In the meantime I wanted to see the kid.

I took my drink and went into his room and sat down on the edge of his bed. His night light was on; I could see I'd woken him. Maybe he'd heard me clinking bottles. Maybe he'd heard us making love.

"Dad," he said.

"Peter."

"Something the matter?"

Peter was twelve. A good kid, a very good kid. He was just eleven when I died. All computers and stereo, back then. Heavy metal and D and D. Sorcerers, dragons, the flaming pits of Hell, the whole bit. And music to match. After I died and came back he got real serious about things, forgot about the rock music and the imaginary Hells. Gave up his friends, too. I was pretty worried about that, and we had a lot of big talks. But he stayed serious. The one thing he stuck with was the computer, only now he used it to map out real Hell. My Hell.

Instead of answering his question I took another drink. He knew what was the matter.

"You going away?" he asked.

I nodded.

"Tell Mom yet?"

"Nope."

He scooted up until he was sitting on his pillow. I could see him thinking: *It was fast this time, Dad. Is it getting faster?* But he didn't say anything.

"Me and your mother," I said. "There's a lot of stuff we didn't get to, this time."

Peter nodded.

"Well—" I began, then stopped. What did he understand? More than I guessed, probably. "Take good care of her," I said.

"Yeah."

I kissed his forehead. I knew how much he hated the smell of liquor, but he managed not to make a face. Good kid, etc.

Then I went in to see his mother.

It was while we were making love that I'd had the first inkling that the change was coming on, but I'd kept it to myself. There wasn't any purpose to ruining the mood; besides, I wasn't sure yet. It wasn't until afterward that I knew for sure.

But I had to tell her now. Another hour or so and I'd be gone.

I sat on the edge of the bed, just like with Peter. Only in this room it was dark. And she wasn't awake. I put my hand on her cheek, felt her breath against my palm. She murmured, and kissed my hand. I squeezed her shoulder until she figured out that I wanted her to wake up.

"Maureen," I said.

"Why aren't you sleeping?"

I wanted to undress again and get back under the covers.

Curl myself around her and fall asleep. Not to say another word. Instead I said: "I'm going back."

"Going back?" Her voice was suddenly hoarse.

I nodded in the dark, but she got the idea.

"Damn you!"

I didn't see the slap coming. That didn't matter, since it wasn't for show. It rattled my teeth. By the time I recovered she was up against the headboard, curled into herself, sobbing weakly.

It wasn't usually this bad for her anymore. She'd numbed the part of herself that felt it the most. But it didn't usually happen this fast, either.

I moved up beside her on the bed, and cradled her head in my hands. Let her cry awhile against my chest. But she wasn't done yet. When she turned her face up it was still raw and contorted with her pain, tendons standing out on her neck.

"Don't say it like that," she gasped out between sobs. "I hate that so much—"

"What?" I tried to say it softly.

"Going *back*. Like that's more real to you now, like that's where you belong, and this is the mistake, the exception—"

I couldn't think of what to say to stop her.

"Oh, God." I held her while she cried some more. "Just don't say it like that, Tom," she said when she could. "I can't stand it."

"I won't say it like that anymore," I said flatly.

She calmed somewhat. We sat still there in the dark, my arms around her.

"I'm sorry," she said, but evenly now. "It's just so fast. Are you sure—"

"Yeah," I said.

"We hardly had any time," she said, sniffling. "I mean, I

was just getting the feeling back, you know? When we were making love. It was so good, just now. Wasn't it?"

"Yes."

"I just thought it was the beginning of a good period again. I thought you'd be back for a while . . . "

I stroked her hair, not saying anything.

"Did you know when we were fucking?" she asked.

"No," I lied. "Not until after."

"I don't know if I can take it anymore, Tom. I can't watch you walk around like a zombie all the time. It's driving me crazy. Every day I look in your eyes, thinking *maybe he's back*, maybe he's about to come back, and you just stare at me. I try to hold your hand in the bed and then you need to scratch yourself or something and you just pull away without saying anything, like you didn't even notice. I can't live like this—"

"I'm sorry," I said, a little hollowly. I wasn't unsympathetic. But we'd been through it before. We always ended in the same place. We always would.

And frankly, once I'd absorbed the impact of her rage, the conversation lost its flavor. My thoughts were beginning to drift ahead, to Hell.

"Maybe you should live somewhere else," she said. "Your body, I mean. When you're not around. You could sleep down at the station or something."

"You know I can't do that."

"Oh no," she said. "I just remembered—"

"What?"

"Your uncle Frank, remember? When does he come?"

"Maybe I'll be back before he shows up," I said. It wasn't likely. I usually spent a week or so in Hell, when I went. Frank was due in four days. "Anyway, he knows about me. There won't be any problem."

4

She sighed. "I just hate having guests when you're gone—"

"Frank's not a guest," I said. "He's family."

She changed the subject. "Did you forget the medication? Maybe if you took the medication—"

"I always take it," I said. "It doesn't work. It doesn't keep me here. You can't take a pill to keep your soul from migrating to Hell."

"It's supposed to help, Tom."

"Well it doesn't matter, does it? I take it. Why do we have to talk about it?"

Now I'd hurt her a little. We were quiet. I felt her composing herself there, in my arms. Making her peace with my going away. Numbing herself.

The result was that we came a little closer together. I was able to share in her calm. We would be nice to each other from here on in. Things were back to normal.

But at the time, we'd backed away from that perilous, agonized place where to be separated by this, or separated at all, even for a minute, was too much to bear; from that place where all that mattered was our love, and where compromise was fundamentally wrong.

Normal was sometimes miles apart.

"You know what I hate the most?" she said. "That I don't even want to stay up with you. You'll only be around for what? A couple of hours more? I should want to get in every last minute. But I don't know what to say to you, really. There's nothing new to say about it. I feel like going to sleep."

"It's coming fast," I said, just to set her straight. "I think it's more like half an hour now."

"Oh," she said.

"But no hard feelings. Go to sleep. I understand."

5

"I have to," she said. "I have to get up in the morning. I feel sick from crying." She slid under the covers and hugged me at the waist. "Tom?" she said, in a smaller voice.

"Maureen."

"Is it getting faster?"

"It's just this one time," I said. "It probably doesn't mean anything. It's just painful to go through—"

"Okay," she said. "I love you, Tom."

"I love you too," I said. "Don't worry."

She went to sleep then, while I lay awake beside her, waiting to cross over.

If Maureen hadn't still been in school when I died, that would have been the end of it. If she hadn't been in debt up to her ears, and still two years away from setting up an office. As it was I had to sit in cold pack for three months while her lawyer pushed the application through. Eventually the courts saw it her way: I was the breadwinner. So they thawed me out.

Now she was supposed to be happy. I kept food on the table, and she had her graduate degree. Her son grew up knowing his dad. It wasn't supposed to matter that my soul shuttled between my living body here on earth, and Hell. She wasn't supposed to complain about that.

Besides, it wasn't my fault.

2

In Hell I'm a small boy.

Younger than Peter. Eight or nine, I'd guess.

I always start in the same place. The beginning is always the same. I'm at that table, in that damned garden, waiting for the witch.

Let me be more specific. I begin as a detail in a tableau:

6

four of us children are seated in a semicircle around a black cast-iron garden table. We sit in matching iron chairs. The lawn beneath us is freshly mowed; the gardener, if there is one, permits dandelions but not crabgrass. At the edge of the lawn is a scrubby border of rosebushes. Beyond that, a forest.

Behind me, when I turn to look, there's a pair of awkward birch saplings. Behind them, the witch's house. Smoke tumbles out of the slate chimney. The witch is supposed to be making us breakfast.

We're supposed to wait. Quietly.

Time is a little slow there, at Hell's entrance. I've waited there with the other children, bickering, playing with the silverware, curling the lace doily under my setting into a tight coil, for what seems like years. Breakfast is never served. Never. The sun, which is hanging just beyond the tops of the trees, never sets. Time stands still there. Which is not to say we sit frozen like statues. Far from it. We're a bunch of hungry children, and we make all kinds of trouble.

But I'm leaving something out.

We sit in a semicircle. That's to make room for the witch's horse. The witch's horse takes up a quarter of the table. He's seated in front of a place like any other guest.

He's waiting for breakfast, too.

The witch's horse is disgusting. The veins under his eyes quiver and he squirms in his seat. His forelegs are chained and staked to keep him at the table. He's sitting on his tail, so he can't swat away the flies which gather and drink at the corners of his mouth. The witch's horse is wearing a rusted pair of cast-iron eyeglass frames on his nose. They're for show, I guess, but they don't fit right. They chafe a pair of raw pink gutters into the sides of his nose.

If I stay at the table and wait for breakfast, subtle changes do occur. Most often the other children get restless, and begin to argue or play, and the table is jostled, and the silverware clatters, and the horse snorts in fear, his yellow eyes leaking. Sometimes a snake or a fox slithers across the lawn and frightens the horse, and he rattles his chains, and the children murmur and giggle. Once a bird flew overhead and splattered oily white birdshit onto the teapot. It was a welcome distraction, like anything else.

Every once in a while the children decide to feel sorry for the horse, and mount a campaign to lure him forward and pluck the glasses from his nose, or daub at his gashes with a wadded-up doily. I tried to help them once, when I was new to Hell. I felt sorry for the horse, too. That was before I saw him and the witch ride together in the forest. When I saw them ride I knew the horse and the witch were in it together.

Seeing them ride, howling and grunting through the trees, is one of the worst things I experience in all of Hell. After the first time I didn't feel sorry for the horse at all.

Whatever the cause, disturbances at the garden table are always resolved the same way. The activity reaches some pitch, the table seems about to overturn, when suddenly there's a sound at the door of the witch's house. We all freeze in our places, breath held. Even the horse knows to sit stock-still, and the only sound that remains is the buzzing of the flies.

We all watch for movement at the door of the witch's house. On the slim hope that maybe, just this once, it's breakfast time. The door opens, just a crack, just enough, and the witch slips out. She's smiling. She's very beautiful, the witch. The most beautiful woman I've ever seen, actually. She's got a great smile. The witch walks out across the lawn, and stops halfway between her door and the table. By now we're all slumped obediently in our seats again. My heart, to be honest, is in my throat.

I'm in love.

"Breakfast will be ready soon," sings the witch. "So just sit quietly, don't bother Horse, and before you know it I'll have something delicious on the table—"

And then she turns and slips back through her doorway and we start all over again.

That's how Hell begins. Maybe if I were a little more patient—waited, say, a thousand years instead of just a hundred—breakfast would appear. But then, knowing Hell, I'm not sure I'd want to see what the witch has been cooking up all this time.

But I don't wait at all anymore. I get up and walk away from the table right away.

Time in Hell doesn't start until you get up from the garden table.

3

The Hell in the computer starts out the same way mine does: in the garden.

Peter laid it all out like Dungeons and Dragons, like a role-playing computer game. We entered a long description of the scene; the other children, the witch's horse, the witch. It was Peter's idea, when I came back with my first tentative reports of what I'd gone through, to map it out with the computer. I think he had the idea that it was like one of his dungeons, and that if we persisted we would eventually find a way out.

So Peter's "Dad" character wakes up at the garden table, same as I do. And when Peter types in a command, like GET UP FROM THE TABLE, WALK NORTH ACROSS THE

LAWN, his "Dad" goes to explore a computer version of the Hell I inhabit.

I don't soft-pedal it. I report what I see, and he enters it into the computer. Factually, we're recreating my Hell. The only thing I spare him are my emotional responses. I omit my fear at what I encounter, my rage at living these moments again and again, my unconscionable lust for the witch . . .

4

When I crossed over that night, after fighting with Maureen, I didn't dawdle at the garden table. I was bored with that by now. I pushed my chair back and started in the direction Peter and I call north; the opposite direction from the witch's house. I ran on my eight-year-old legs across the lawn, through a gap in the border of rose-bushes, and into the edge of the forest.

The north was my favored direction at the moment, because I'd explored it the least. Oh, Hell goes on forever in every direction, of course. But I don't always get very far. I explored the territories nearest the witch's garden most thoroughly, in any direction; as I get farther out it gets less and less familiar. I just don't always get very far out.

And the nearby territories to the north somehow seemed less *hackneyed* to me at the moment.

The forest to the north quickly gives way to an open field. It's called the Field of Tubers, because of the knuckled roots that grow there. Sort of like carrots, or potatoes, or knees. Like carrots in that they're orange, like potatoes in the way the vines link them all together, under the ground. Like knees, or elbows, in the way they twitch, and bleed when you kick them.

The first few times I came to the Field of Tubers I tried to run across. Now I walk, slowly, carefully. That way I avoid falling into the breeding holes. The holes don't look like much if you don't step on them; just little circular holes, like wet anthills in the dirt. They throb a little. But if your foot lands on them they gape open, the entrance stretching like a mouth, and you fall in.

The breeding holes are about four feet deep, and muddy. Inside, the newborn tubers writhe in heaps. They're not old enough to take root yet. It's a mess.

Sure, you can run across the field, scrambling back out of the breeding holes, scraping the crushed tubers off the bottom of your shoes. You get to the other side of the field either way. It's not important. Myself, I walk.

Time, which is frozen at the witch's breakfast table, starts moving once I enter the forest. But time in Hell takes a very predictable course. The sun, which has been sitting at the top of the trees, refusing to set, goes down as I cross the Field of Tubers. It's night when I reach the other side, no matter how long it takes me to cross. If I run, looking back over my shoulder, I can watch the sun plummet through the treetops and disappear. Of course, if I run looking back over my shoulder I trip over the tubers and fall into the breeding holes constantly. If I idle in the field, squatting at the edge of a breeding hole, poking it with my finger to watch it spasm open, the sun refuses to set.

But why would I ever want to do that?

5

When I first came back, when they warmed me up and put me back together, they didn't send me home right away. I had to spend a week in an observation ward, and on the fourth day they sent a doctor in to let me know where I stood.

"You'll be fine," he said. "You won't have any trouble holding down your job. Most people won't know the difference. But you will cross over."

"I've heard," I said.

"It shouldn't affect your public life," he said. "You'll be able to carry on most conversations in a perfunctory way. You just won't seem very interested in personal questions. Your mind will appear to be wandering. And you won't be very affectionate. Your co-workers won't notice, but your wife will."

"I won't want to fuck her," I said.

"No, you won't."

"Okay," I said. "How often will I go?"

"That varies from person to person. Some get lucky, and cross over just once or twice for the rest of their lives. It's rare, but it does happen. At the other extreme, some spend most of their time over there. For most, it's somewhere in between."

"You're not saying anything."

"That's right; I'm not. But I should say that how often you cross over isn't always as important as how you handle it. The stress of not knowing is as bad or worse than actually going through it. The anticipation. It can cast a pall over the times when you're back. A lot of marriages . . . don't survive the resurrection."

"And there's no way to change it."

"Not really. You'll get a prescription for Valizax. It's a hormone that stimulates the secretions of a gland associated, in some studies, with the migration. Some people claim it helps, and maybe it does, in their cases. Or maybe it's just a placebo effect. And then there's therapy."

"Therapy?"

"They'll give you the brochure when you leave. There are several support groups for migrators. Some better than others. We recommend one in particular. It's grounded in solid psychoanalytic theory, and like the drug, some people have said it improves the condition. But that's not for me to say."

I went to the support group. The good one. Once. I don't know what I was expecting. There were seven or eight people there that night, and the group counselor, who I learned wasn't resurrected, had never made the trips back and forth from his own Hell. After some coffee and uneasy socializing we went and sat in a circle. They went around, bringing each other up to date on their progress, and the counselor handed out brownie points for every little epiphany. When they got to me, they wanted to hear about my Hell.

Only they didn't call it Hell. They called it a "psychic landscape." And I quickly learned that they wanted me to consider it symbolic. The counselor wanted me to explain what my Hell *meant*.

I managed to contain my anger, but I left at the first break. Hell doesn't *mean* anything. Excuse me—*my* Hell doesn't mean anything. Maybe yours does.

But mine doesn't. That's what makes it Hell.

And it's not symbolic. It's very, very real.

6

On the other side of the Field of Tubers, if I go straight over the crest, is the Grove of the Robot Maker. A dense patch of trees nestled at the base of a hill.

The moon is up by this time.

The robot maker is an old man. A tired old man. He putters around in the grove in a welder's helmet, but he never welds. His robots are put together with wire and tinsnips. They're mostly pathetic. Half of them barely make it up to the Battle Pavilion before collapsing. He made better ones, once, if you believe him. He's badly in need of a young apprentice.

That's where I come in.

"Boy, you're here," he says when I arrive. He hands me a pliers or a ball-peen hammer. "Let me show you what I'm working on," he says. "I'll let you help." He tries to involve me in his current project, whatever it is. Whatever heap of refuse he's currently animating.

His problem, which he describes to me at length, is that his proudest creation, Colonel Eagery, went renegade on his way up to the Battle Pavilion. Back when the robot maker was young and strong and built robots with fantastic capabilities. Colonel Eagery, he says, was his triumph, but the triumph went sour. The robot rebelled, and set up shop on the far side of the mountains, building evil counterparts to the robot maker's creations. The strong, evil robots that so routinely demolish the robot maker's own robots out on the Battle Pavilion.

I have two problems with this story.

First of all, I know Colonel Eagery, and he isn't a robot. Oh no. I know all too well that Eagery, who I also call The Happy Man, is flesh and blood.

The second is that the robot maker is too old and feeble for me to imagine that he's ever been able to build anything capable and effective at all, let alone something as capable and effective as I know Eagery to be.

Besides, Hell doesn't have a *before*. Hell is stuck in time, repeating endlessly. Hell doesn't have a past. It just *is*. The robot maker is always old and ineffectual, and he always has been.

But I never say this. My role is just as predetermined as the robot maker's. I humor him. When I'm passing through this part of Hell, I'm the robot maker's apprentice. I make a show of interest in his latest project. I help him steer it up to the Battle Pavilion. I can't say why. That's just the way things are in this corner of Hell.

This time, when I entered the grove, I found the robot maker already heading up toward the pavilion. He'd built a little robot terrier this time. It was surprisingly mobile and lively, yipping and snapping at the robot maker's heels. I fell in with them, and the robot maker put his heavy, dry hand on my shoulder. The mechanical terrier sniffed at my shoes and barked once, then ran ahead, rooting frantically in the moss.

"He's a good one, boy," said the robot maker. "I think he's got a bit of your spark in him. This one's got a fighting chance against whatever the Colonel's got cooked up."

It didn't, of course. I couldn't bring myself to look at the poor little mechanical terrier. It was about to be killed. But I didn't say anything.

At this point in our hike through the grove the witch and the witch's horse ride by. It's another dependable part of my clockwork Hell. They turn up at about this point in my journey—the moon just up, a breeze stirring—whichever direction I choose. It's a horrible sight, but it's one I've gotten used to. Like just about everything else.

The horse is a lot more imposing freed from his stakes at the table. He's huge and sweaty and hairy, his nostrils dilated wide, his lips curled back. He's not wearing those funny glasses anymore. The witch rides him cowboy style, bareback. She bends her head down and grunts exhortations into the horse's ear. She's still beautiful, I guess. And I still love her—sort of. I feel mixed up about the witch when she rides, actually. A combination of fear and pity and shame. An odd sense that she wouldn't do it if she didn't somehow *have* to. That the horse is somehow doing it to her.

But mostly I'm just afraid. As they rode through the grove now, I stood frozen in place with fear, just like the first time.

The robot maker did what he always does: covered my eyes with his bony hand and muttered, "Terrible, terrible! Not in front of the boy!"

I peered through his fingertips, compelled to watch.

And then they were gone, snorting away into the night, and we were alone in the grove again. The terrier yipped after them angrily. The robot maker shook his head, gripped my shoulder, and we walked on.

The pavilion sits on a plateau at the edge of the woods. The base is covered with trees, invisible until you're there. The battle area, up on top, is like a ruined Greek temple. The shattered remains of the original roof are piled around the edges. The pavilion itself is littered with the glowing, radio-active shambles of the robot maker's wrecked creations. The pavilion is so infused with radiation that normal physics don't apply there; some of the ancient robots still flicker back into flame when the wind picks up, and sometimes one of the wrecks goes into an accelerated decline and withers into ashes, as though years of entropy have finally caught up with it. The carcasses tell the story of the robot maker's decline; his recent robots are less ambitious and formidable, and their husks are correspondingly more pathetic. Many of the newer ones simply failed on their way to the pavilion; their ruined bodies litter the pathway up the hill.

But not the terrier. He bounded up the hill ahead of us, reached the crest, and disappeared over the top. The robot maker and I hurried after him, not wanting him to lose his match before we even saw what he was fighting.

His opponent was a wolfman robot. As from an old horror movie, his face was more human than dog. It was a perfect example of how the robot maker's creations were so badly overmatched: what chance does a house pet have against a wolfman? It was often like this, a question of several degrees of sophistication.

Standing on two feet, the wolfman towered over the terrier. He spoke too, taunting the little dog, who could only yip and growl in response.

"Here, boy," cackled the wolfman. "Come on, pup. Come to daddy. Here we go." He gestured beckoningly. The terrier barked and reared back. "Come on, boy. Jeez." He looked to us for sympathy as we approached. "Lookit this. Here boy, I'm not gonna hurt you. I'm not gonna hurt you. I'm just gonna wring your fucking neck. Come on. COME HERE YOU GODDAMN LITTLE PIECE OF SHIT!"

The wolfman lunged, scrambling down and seizing the terrier by the neck, and took a bite on the forearm for his trouble. I heard metal grate on metal. "Ow! Goddammit. That does it." He throttled the little robot, which squealed until its voice was gone. "This is gonna hurt me more than it hurts you," said the wolfman, even as he tossed the broken scrap-metal carcass aside. The robot maker and I just stood, staring in stupid wonder.

"Ahem," said the wolfman, picking himself up. "Boy. Where was I? Oh, well. Some other fucking time." He turned his back and walked away, clearing his throat, picking imaginary pieces of lint from his body, tightening an imaginary tie like Rodney Dangerfield.

As soon as the wolfman was over the edge of the pavilion

and out of sight, the robot maker ran to his ruined terrier and threw his skeletal body over it in sorrow, as though he could shield it from some further indignity. I turned away. I hated the robot maker's weeping. I didn't want to have to comfort him again. The sight of it, frankly, made me sick. It was one of Hell's worst moments. Besides, hanging around the pavilion weeping over his failures was how the robot maker had soaked up so much radiation, and gotten so old. If I stuck around I might get like him.

I snuck away.

7

A few months after my brush with the support group I met another migrator in a bar.

I'd come back from Hell that afternoon, at work. I rein-habitated my body while I was sitting behind the mike, reading out a public service announcement. For once I kept my cool; didn't tell anyone at the station, didn't call Maureen at home. I stopped at the bar on my way home, just to get a few minutes for myself before I let Maureen and Peter know I was back.

I got talking to the guy at my right. I don't remember how, but it came out that he was a migrator, too. Just back, like me. We started out boozily jocular, then got quiet as we compared notes, not wanting to draw attention to ourselves, not wanting to trigger anyone's prejudices.

He told me about his Hell, which was pretty crazy. The setting was urban, not rural. He started out on darkened city streets, chased by Chinamen driving garbage trucks and shooting at him with pistols. There was a nuclear war; the animals mutated, grew intelligent and vicious. It went on from there.

I told him about mine, and then I told him about the support group and what I'd thought of it.

"Shit, yes," he said. "I went through that bullshit. Don't let them try to tell you what you're going through. They don't know shit. They can't know what we go through. They aren't *there*, man."

I asked him how much of his time he spent in Hell.

"Sheeeit. I'm not back here one day for every ten I spend *there*. I work in a bottling plant, man. Quality control. I look at bottles all day, then I go out drinking with a bunch of other guys from the plant. Least that's what they tell me. When I come back I don't even *know* those guys. Buncha strangers. When I come back"—he raised his glass—"I go out drinking alone."

I asked him about his wife. He finished his drink and ordered another one before he said anything.

"She got sick of waiting around, I guess," he said. "I don't blame her. Least she got me brought back. I owe her *that*."

We traded phone numbers. He wasn't exactly the kind of guy I'd hang around with under ordinary circumstances, but as it was we had a lot in common.

I called a few times. His answering machine message was like this: "Sorry, I don't seem to be *home* right now. Leave a message at the tone and I'll call you as soon as I'm *back*."

Maureen told me he called me a few times, too. Always while I was away.

8

When I leave the robot maker at the pavilion, I usually continue north, to the shrunken homes in the Garden of Razor Blades. The garden begins on the far side of the pavilion. A thicket of trees, at the entrance, only the trees are leafed with razor blades. The moonlight is reflected off a thousand tiny mirrors; it's quite pretty, really. The forest floor is layered with fallen razor blades. They never rust, because it never rains in Hell.

The trees quickly give way to a delicately organized garden laced with paths, and the bushes and flowers, like the trees before them, are covered with razor blades. The paths wend around to a clearing, and in the middle of the clearing are the shrunken homes. They're built into a huge dirt mound, like a desert mesa inhabited by Indians, or a gigantic African anthill. Hundreds of tiny doorways and windows are painstakingly carved out of the mound. Found objects are woven into the structure; shirt buttons, safety pins, eyeglass frames, and nail clippers. But no razor blades.

The shrunken humans are just visible as I approach. Tiny figures in little cloth costumes, busily weaving or cooking or playing little ball games on the roofs and patios of the homes. I never get any closer than that before the storm hits.

It's another part of Hell's program. The witch storm rises behind the trees just as I enter the clearing. The witch storm is a tiny, self-contained hurricane, on a scale, I suppose, to match the shrunken homes. A black whirlwind about three times my size. It's a rainless hurricane, an entity of wind and dust that roils into action without warning and sends the shrunken humans scurrying for cover inside the mound.

With good reason. The storm tears razor blades from the treetops and off the surface of the paths and sends them into a whirling barrage against the sides of the shrunken homes. By the time the storm finishes, what was once a detailed, intricate miniature civilization is reduced to an undifferentiated heap of dust and dirt.

There's nothing I can do to stop it. I tried at first. Planted myself between the shrunken homes and the witch storm and tried to fend it off. What I got for my trouble was a rash of tiny razor cuts on my arms and face. By the time the storm retreated I'd barely protected a square foot of the mound from the assault.

The storm is associated with the witch. Don't ask me why. There are times, though, when I think I see a hint of her figure in its whirling form.

If I forget the mound and run for cover I can usually avoid feeling the brunt of it. Running away, I might take a few quick cuts across the shoulders or the backs of my legs, but that's it.

This time I ran so fast I barely took a cut. I ducked underneath a bush that was already stripped clean of blades; its branches protected me. I listened as the storm ravaged the mound, then faded away. A smell of ozone was in the air.

When I looked up again, I was looking into the face of Colonel Eagery. The Happy Man.

9

The only thing that's not predictable in Hell, the only thing that doesn't happen according to some familiar junction of time and locale, is the appearance of The Happy Man. He's a free operator. He's his own man. He comes and goes as he pleases, etc.

He's also my ticket home.

When Colonel Eagery is done with me I go back. Back to home reality, back to Maureen and Peter and the radio station where I work. I get to live my life again. No matter where he appears, no matter which tableau he disturbs, Eagery's appearance means I get to go back.

After he's done with me.

Before I left the support group the counselor—the one

who'd never even been to Hell—told me to focus on what he called the "reentry episode." He told me that the situation that triggered return was usually the key to Hell, the source of the unresolved tension. The idea, he said, was to identify the corresponding episode in your own past.

I could only laugh.

There's nothing in my life to correspond to Eagery. There couldn't be. Eagery is the heart of my Hell. He's Hell itself. If there had been anything in my life to even approximate The Happy Man, I wouldn't be here to tell you about it. I'd be a wimpering, sniveling wreck in a straightjacket somewhere. Nothing I've encountered in the real world comes close.

Not in *my* reality.

Frankly, if something in the real world corresponds to Colonel Eagery, I don't want to know about it.

10

The Happy Man lifted me over his shoulder and carried me out of the Garden of Razor Blades, into the dark heart of the woods. When we got to a quiet moonlit grove, he set me down.

"There you go, Tom," he said, dusting himself off. He's the only one in Hell who knows my name. "Boy, what a scene. Listen, let's keep it to ourselves, what do you say? Our little secret, okay? A midnight rondee voo."

The Happy Man is always urgently conspiratorial. It's a big priority with him. I feel I should oblige him, though I'm not always sure what he's referring to. I nodded now.

"Yeah." He slapped me on the back, a little too hard. "You and me, the midnight riders, huh? Lone Ranger and Tonto. What do you mean 'we,' white man? Heh. I told you that one? It's like this . . . "

He told me a long, elaborate joke which I failed to understand. Nonetheless, I sat cross-legged in the clearing, rapt.

At the end he laughed for both of us, a loud, sloppy sound that echoed in the trees. "Oh yeah," he said, wiping a tear from his eye. "Listen, you want some candy? Chocolate or something?" He rustled in a kit bag. "Or breakfast. It's still pretty early. I bet that goddamned witch didn't feed you kids any breakfast, did she?" He took out a bowl and a spoon, then poured in milk and dry cereal from a cardboard box.

The cereal, when I looked, consisted of little puffed and sugar-coated penises, breasts, and vaginas, floating innocently in the milk.

I tried not to gag, or let him see I was having any trouble getting it down. I wanted to please Colonel Eagery, wanted to let him know I was thankful. While I ate he whistled, and unpacked the neckties from his bag.

I watched, curious. "You like these?" he said, holding them up. "Yeah. You'll get to wear them someday. Look real sharp, too. Like your dad. World-beater, that's what you feel like in a necktie." He began knotting them together to make a set of ropes, then looped them around the two nearest trees. "Here," he said, handing me one end. "Pull on this. Can you pull it loose?"

I put down the bowl of cereal and tugged on the neckties.

"Can you? Pull harder."

I shook my head.

"Yeah, they're tough all right. Don't worry about it, though. Your dad couldn't break it either. That's American craftsmanship." He nodded at the cereal. "You done with that? Yeah? C'mere."

I went.

This is my curse: I trust him. Every time. I develop

skepticism about the other aspects of Hell; the witch's overdue breakfast, the robot maker's pathetic creations, but Colonel Eagery I trust every time. I am made newly innocent.

"Here," he said. "Hold this." He put one end of the rope in my right hand, and began tying the other end to my left. "Okay." He moved to the right. "What do you mean we, white man? Heh. Cowboys and Indians, Tom. Lift your leg up here—that's a boy. Okay." He grunts over the task of binding me, legs splayed between the two trees. "You an Indian, Tom? Make some noise and let's see."

I started crying.

"Oh, no, don't do that," said The Happy Man, gravely. "Show the Colonel that you're a good sport, for chrissakes. Don't be a *girl*. You'll—ruin all the fun." His earnestness took me by surprise; I felt guilty. I didn't want to ruin anyone's fun. So I managed to stop crying. "That's it, Tommy. Chin up." It wasn't easy, lying there like a low-slung hammock in the dirt, my arms stretched over my head, to put my chin up. I decided it would be enough to smile. "There you go," said Eagery. "God, you're pretty."

The last knot secured, he turned away to dig in his bag, and emerged with a giant, clownish pair of scissors. I squirmed, but couldn't get away. He inserted the blade in my pants cuff and began snipping apart the leg of the corduroys. "Heigh ho! Don't move, Tom. You wouldn't want me to clip something off here, would you?" He quickly scissored up both sides, until my pants were hanging in shreds from my outstretched legs, then snipped the remaining link, so they fell away. A few quick strokes of the scissors and he'd eliminated my jockey shorts too. "Huh." He tossed the scissors aside and ran his hands up my legs. "Boy, that's smooth. Like a baby."

24

When he caressed me I got hard, despite my fear.

"Okay. Okay. That feel good? Aw, look at that." He was talking to himself now. A steady patter which he kept up over the sound of my whimpering. "Look here Tom, I got one too. *Big*-size. Daddy-size." He straddled me. "Open up for the choo-choo, Tommy. Uh."

I didn't pass out this time until he flipped me over, my arms and legs twisted, my stomach and thighs pressed into the dirt. Blackness didn't come until then.

Then I crossed back over.

Another safe passage back from Hell, thanks again to The Happy Man.

11

If anyone at the station had questions about my behavior, they kept to themselves.

I came back on mike again. "—bumper to bumper down to the Dumbarton . . . " I trailed away in the middle of the traffic report and punched in a commercial break on cart. "Anyone got something to drink?" I said into the station intercom.

"I think there's some beer in the fridge," said Andrew, the support technician on shift, poking his head into the studio.

"Keep this going," I said, and left. He could run a string of ads, or punch in one of our prerecorded promos. It wasn't a major deviation.

The station fridge was full of rotting, half-finished lunches and pint cartons of sour milk, plus a six-pack of lousy beer. It wasn't Johnnie Walker, but it would do. I needed to wash the memory of Eagery's flesh out of my mouth.

I leaned against the wall of the lounge and quietly, methodically, downed the beer.

The programming was piped into the lounge and I listened as Andrew handled my absence. He loaded in a stupid comedy promo; the words "Rock me" from about a million old songs, spliced together into a noisy barrage. Then his voice came over the intercom. "Lenny's down here, Tom. Take off if you want."

I didn't need a second hint. In ten minutes I was trapped in the bumper to bumper myself, listening to the station on my car radio.

Maureen's car wasn't in the driveway when I pulled up. She was still at work. No reason to hurry home if she thought I was still away, I suppose. But the lights were on. Peter was home. And, as it turned out, so was Uncle Frank. I'd forgotten about the visit, but while I was away he'd set up in the guest room.

He and Peter were sitting together in front of the computer, playing Hell. They looked up when I came in, and Peter recognized the change in the tone of my voice right away. Smart kid.

"Hey, Dad." He made a show of introducing us, so Frank would understand that there was a change. "Dad, Uncle Frank's here."

Frank and I shook hands.

I hadn't seen my father's brother for seven or eight years, and in that time he'd aged decades. He was suddenly a gray old man. It made me wonder how my father would look if he were still around.

"Tommy," Frank said. "It's been a long time." His voice was as faded and weak as everything else. I could hear him trying to work out the difference between me now and the zombie version he'd been living with for the past few days.

I didn't let him wonder for too long. I gave his hand a

good squeeze, and then I put my arms around him. I needed the human contact anyway, after Hell.

"I need a drink," I said. "Frank?" I cocked my head toward the living room. Uncle Frank nodded.

The kid got the drift on his own. "I'll see you later, Dad." He turned back to his computer, made a show of being involved.

I led Frank to the couch and poured us both a drink.

Though I hadn't seen him since before I died, Uncle Frank knew all about my situation. We wrote letters, and every once in a while spoke on the phone. Frank had never married, and after my father died he and I were one another's only excuse for "family." He wasn't well off, but he'd wired Maureen some cash when I died. In his letters he'd been generous, too, sympathetic and unsuperstitious. In my letters I'd unloaded a certain measure of my guilt and shame at what my resurrection had done to the marriage, and he was always understanding. But I could see now that he had to make an effort, in person, not to appear uncomfortable. He'd been living with my soulless self for a few days, and his eyes told me that he needed to figure out who he was talking to now.

For my part, I was making an adjustment to the changes in Frank. In my memory he was permanently in his forties, a more garrulous and eccentric version of my father. Frank had been the charismatic oddball in the family, never without a quip, never quite out of the doghouse, but always expansive and charming. I'd often thought that my falsely genial on-radio persona was based on a pale imitation of Frank. Only now he just seemed tired and old.

"You've got a nice setup here, Tom," he said quietly.

"That's Maureen's work," I said. "She busts her ass keeping it all together."

Frank nodded. "I've seen."

"How long you staying with us?"

Now Frank snickered in a way that recalled, if only faintly, the man I remembered. "How long you have me?"

"You don't need to be back?" How Frank made his living had always been unclear. He'd been a realtor at some point, then graduated to the nebulous status of "consultant." Professional bullshitter was always my hunch.

But now he said, "I'm not going back. I think I want to set up out here for a while."

"Well, for my part you're welcome to stick around until you find a place," I said. He'd sounded uncomfortable, and I decided not to pry. "It's really up to Maureen, you understand. The burden's on her—"

"Oh, I've been helping out," he said quickly. "I've become quite a chef, actually . . . "

The way he trailed away told me I'd probably already eaten several of his meals. "I'm sure," I said. There was a pause. "Listen, Frank, let's break the ice. I don't remember shit about what happens while I'm away. Treat me like a newborn babe when I come back. One who nurses on a whiskey tumbler."

I watched him relax. He lowered his eyes and said, "I'm sorry, Tom. I haven't been around family, I mean *real* family, for so long. It's got me thinking about the past. You know . . . " He looked up sharply. "You're a grown man. Have been for a long time. But your dad and your mom and you as a little kid, me coming to visit—that's how I remember you. Always will, I think."

"I understand." I worked on my whiskey.

"Anyway—" He waved his hand dismissively. "It's good to see you finally. Good to see the three of you together, making it go."

"I'm glad it looks good." I could only be honest. "It isn't always easy."

"Oh, I didn't mean, I mean, yes. Of course. And anything, any little thing I can do to help—" He watched my eyes for reaction, looking terribly uncomfortable. "And Tom?"

I nodded.

"I already mentioned this to Maureen and Peter. Uh, you don't seem to pick up the phone when you're away, but now that you're back—"

"Yes?"

"If you do pick up the phone, if anyone calls, *I'm not here*, okay?"

"Sure, Frank."

"I just need to create a little distance right now," he said obscurely.

I wasn't sure whether to press him on the point. My chance was taken away, anyway, by Maureen's arrival. She walked in and peered at us over the top of a couple of bags of groceries, then took them on into the kitchen without saying a word. She knew I was back. The drink in my hand told her all she needed to know.

Frank got up and hurried into the kitchen behind her. I heard him insist on putting away the groceries by himself.

Then Maureen came out. I put my drink on the coffee table and stood up and we stood right next to each other, close without quite touching for a long time. Quiet, knowing that when words came, things might get too complicated again. In the background I could hear Frank putting the groceries into the fridge and the gentle, hurried tapping of Peter's fingers on his keyboard.

Maureen and I sat on the couch and kissed.

"Hey," came Frank's voice eventually. "Pete and I were talking about catching a movie or something. We could get a slice of pizza too, take the car and be back in a few hours—"

"Peter?" I said.

He appeared in the doorway, right on cue. "Yeah, Dad, there's a new Clive Barker movie—"

"Homework?"

"Didn't get any."

I gave Frank the car keys and twenty bucks for pizza or whatever. I was being tiptoed around, sure, but I didn't let myself feel patronized. The few breaks I get I earn, twice over.

They left, and Maureen and I went back to kissing on the couch. We still hadn't exchanged a word. After a while we went into the bedroom like that, affectionate, silent. We didn't get around to words until an hour or so later.

Turned out it was just as well.

12

Maureen had closed her eyes and rolled over on her side, curled against me. But the muscles of her mouth were tight; she wasn't asleep. I put my hand in her hair and said her name. She said mine.

"How's it been?" I said.

She waited a while before answering. "I don't know, Tom. Okay, I guess."

"I wasn't gone too long this time," I said, though it didn't need saying.

She sighed. "That last one just took something out of me."

"What are you saying?"

She spoke quietly, tonelessly, into the crook of my arm. "I don't know how long you'll be around. I can't trust it anymore. I feel like if I let myself relax I'll get ripped off again."

There wasn't any answer to that, so I shut up and let the subject drop. "Peter all right?"

"Yes. Always. He's going to be on some debating thing now. I think he likes having Frank around."

"Do you?"

She didn't answer the question. "He's so different from when I first met him, Tom. When we got married. I thought he was such a buffoon. Such a loud, intrusive character." She laughed. "I was afraid we'd have a son like him. Now he's so *polite*."

"He's a guest in your house," I pointed out.

"It's not just that," she said. "He's gotten old, I guess."

"He said he's been cooking. Is he in your way? He'll go if I tell him to."

"He wants to move out here. Did he tell you that?"

"Yes," I said. And thought, *As well as something odd about the telephone*. I didn't say it. "But he's got money, I think. We'll find him a place—" I stopped. She still hadn't said whether she wanted him around, and the gap was beginning to irritate me. I was sensitive enough to her by now that I noticed what wasn't being said.

And she was smart enough to notice my irritation.

"He's fine, really," she said quickly. "He's actually quite a help, cooking . . . "

"Yes?"

"I've just gotten used to being alone, Tom. With you gone, and Peter out with his friends. I've had a lot of freedom."

The skin on my back began to crawl. I took my hand out of her hair.

"Say it," I said.

She sighed. "I'm trying to. I've been lonely, Tom. And I don't mean lonely for some odd old relative of yours to sleep in the guest room, either."

"Is it someone I know?"

"No."

I thought I could manage a couple more questions before I blew my cool. "Does Peter know?"

"No."

"*Are you sure?*"

"Jesus, Tom. Yes, I'm sure."

"What about Frank?"

"What about him? I didn't tell him. I can't imagine how he'd guess."

"There aren't any letters, then. Or weird phone calls. You aren't being sloppy—"

"No, Tom."

That was all I could take. In pretty much one motion I got up and put on my pants. Almost burst a blood vessel buttoning my shirt.

Then I surprised myself: I didn't hit her.

Instead I put on my shoes and went to the kitchen for a bottle, and sat down on the couch in the moonlight and drank.

It wasn't any good. I couldn't be in the house. I put on a jacket and took the bottle for a walk around the neighborhood.

13

To the west, in my Hell, there's a place I call the Ghost Town. It's like a Western movie set, with cheap facades passing for buildings, and if anyone lives there, they're hiding. The moon lights the main street from behind a patch of trees, throwing cigarette butts and crumpled foil wrappers discarded there into high relief. Sometimes I can make out hoofprints in the dust.

In the middle of the street is a naked, crying baby.

Gusts of wind rise as I walk through the Ghost Town, and they grow stronger as I approach the baby, whipping the dust and refuse of the street into its face. The baby's crying chokes into a cough, sputters, then resumes, louder than before. The baby is cold. I can tell; I'm cold myself, there in the Ghost Town. By the time I reach down to pick up the baby, the wind tearing through my little chest, I'm seeking its warmth as much as offering my own.

If I pick up the baby it turns into The Happy Man. Instantly. Every time.

I've already said what happens when The Happy Man appears.

Needless to say, then, I avoid the Ghost Town. I steer a wide berth around it. I often avoid the west altogether. As much as I want to go back to my life, I can't bring myself to pick up the baby, knowing that I'm bringing on Colonel Eagery. I'm not capable of it. And I'm not comfortable walking through that town, feeling the rising wind and listening to the baby's cries, and not doing anything. Hell seems so contingent on my actions; maybe if I don't go in that direction there isn't a baby in the first place. I'd like to think so.

Anyway, it had been months since I'd walked through the Ghost Town.

But I walked through it that night, in my dreams. I don't know why.

14

I woke up still dressed and clutching the bottle, on the living room couch. What woke me was the noise in the kitchen. Maureen making breakfast for Peter.

Head low, I slunk past the kitchen doorway and into the bedroom.

By the time I woke again Peter was off to school, and Maureen was out too, at work. I put myself through the shower, then called the station and said I wasn't coming in. They took it all right.

When I went back out I found Uncle Frank making coffee, enough for two. I accepted a cup and grunted my thanks.

"Can you handle some eggs?" he asked. "There's an omelet I've been meaning to try. You can be my guinea pig . . . "

I cleared my throat. "Uh, sure," I said.

He went into action while I let the coffee work on my mood. I was impressed, actually. Frank seemed to have diverted some of his eccentric passion into cookery. He knew how to use all the wedding-present stuff that Maureen and I had let gather dust. The smells charmed me halfway out of my funk.

"Here we go." He juggled it out of the pan and onto a plate, sprinkled some green stuff on top and put it in front of me. I waited for him to cut it in half, and when he didn't I said, "What about you?"

"Oh," he said. "I ate before. Please."

I put the whole thing away without any trouble. Frank sipped his coffee and watched while I ate.

"I used to cook for you when you were a little boy," he said. " 'Course then it was eggs in bacon grease, smeared with catsup—"

My throat suddenly tightened in a choking spasm. I spurted coffee and bits of egg across the table, almost into Frank's lap. He got up and slapped at my back, but by then it was over.

"Jeez," I said. "Some kind of hangover thing. I'm sorry . . . "

"Relax, Tom." He got me a glass of water. "Probably the memory of those old breakfasts . . . " He laughed.

"Yeah." *Or the thought of Maureen and her new pal in the sack.* I didn't say it, though. I suddenly felt intense shame. Frank represented my family, he stood in for my dad. I didn't want him to know the reason for my bender.

"Listen, Tom," he said. "What say we go down to the water today? That's not a long drive, is it?"

"Sounds great," I admitted. "I need to get out of the house."

An hour later we parked out by the Marina and walked down to the strip of beach. I expected Uncle Frank to tire quickly; instead I had to hurry to keep up. I felt like I was seeing him slowly come back to life, first in the kitchen, concocting the omelet, and now out here on the beach. He seemed to sense the deadness and emptiness in me and tried valiantly to carry on both ends of a chatty conversation. I heard glimpses of the old raconteur in his voice, which only made me wonder more what had sent it into hiding in the first place.

"Frank," I said, when he came to the end of a story, "what happened? What's got you on the run?"

He took a deep breath and looked out over the water. "I was hoping that wouldn't come up, Tom. I don't want to get you or Maureen into it."

"I'll decide what I want to get into," I said. "Besides, it doesn't necessarily protect us to keep us in the dark."

He turned and looked me in the eye. "That's a point. It's— it's the Mob, Tom. Only it's not so simple anymore, to just say Mob. There's a blurry territory where it crosses over into some federal agency . . . Anyway, it's enough to say that I got crossed up with some real bad guys. I screwed 'em on some property." He was looking out to sea again, and I couldn't read his expression. "I'm not sure how much they really care, or how long before they get distracted by something else. Could be they just wanted to throw a scare at me. I just know it felt like time to get out of town for a while."

"God, Frank. I'm sorry. That sounds tough."

"Ah, it's all my own goddamn fault. Anyway, I won't stay much longer at your place. I would have gone already if you weren't—you know, away. And Pete seemed—I don't know. I felt like I could be of some use. It took my mind off my own problems."

"Stay as long as you like, Frank."

He smiled grimly. "I'm not necessarily in the right, you know . . . "

"Don't bother," I said. "When you go through some of the shit I've gone through, it gives you a different perspective. Right isn't always a relevant concept. You're family."

He turned and looked at me, then. Hard. Suddenly he wasn't just my clichéd notion of "Uncle Frank" anymore; he was a complex, intelligent, and not always easy to comprehend man whom I'd known since before I could remember. Maybe it was just my emotional state, but for a moment I was terrified.

"Thanks, Tom."

"Uh, don't mention it."

We looked out over the water without saying anything.

"I'm hip to Maureen," said Frank after a while.

I probably tightened my fists in my pockets, but that was it.

"There isn't really anything to say," he went on. "Just that you've got my sympathy."

"Don't hold it against her," I said. "I make it pretty tough. My whole setup makes it pretty tough."

"Yeah."

36

"Have you met him?" I asked.

"Nope. Just a phone call I wasn't supposed to hear. Not her fault. My ears tend to prick up at the sound of the phone right now."

"Peter?"

"Jeez. I don't think so, Tom. Not that I know of. But he's a smart kid."

"No kidding."

We came to a high place over the water, with a concrete platform and a rusted steel railing. I leaned on it and smelled the mist. Birds wheeled overhead. I thought about the night before, and wondered what I was going to say to Maureen the next time I saw her.

After a while I guess I choked up a little. "God damn," I said. "I didn't even get to see my kid last night."

"That's not your fault," said Frank quietly.

"I always hang out with the kid, Frank. I'm never so wrapped up in my goddamned problems that I don't have time for him. I only just got back."

Frank got a cheerleader tone in his voice again. "Let's go pick him up at school," he said. "Smart guy like him can miss half a day."

"I don't know."

"C'mon. It's easy. You just show up and they turn him over. Big treat, makes him a celebrity with all his pals."

"You do this a lot?"

Frank got serious. "Uh, no," he said. He almost sounded offended, for no reason I could discern. "They'd never turn the child over to anyone but his mother or father." He turned away, the mood between us suddenly and inexplicably sour.

"Something the matter?" I said.

He closed his eyes for a minute. "Sorry, Tom. I guess I just all of a sudden got an image of my friends from back east showing up at the schoolyard. I'm just being paranoid . . . "

We exchanged a long look.

"Let's go," I said.

15

It was a relief to learn what a pain in the ass it was to get a kid out of school halfway through the day. We had to fill out a visitor's form just to go to the office, and then we had to fill out another form to get permission to yank Peter from class, and then a secretary walked us to the classroom anyway.

It turned out it was a computer class. A bunch of the kids there had played Peter's software Hell, which made me a visiting celebrity. I had to shake a lot of little hands to get back out. Frank was right: the visit would make Peter the most popular kid in school tomorrow.

We went out for hamburgers downtown, then we went back home. If Peter was disturbed by my drunken sprawl on the couch that morning, he did a good job of covering it up. He and Frank were full of computer talk, and I could see how well they were getting along.

Eventually we got around to the traditional post-Hell update, Peter and I huddled at the computer, punching in whatever new information I'd picked up on my trip. This time Frank sat in.

"Robot maker built a terrier," I said. "A little livelier than the usual crap . . . " Peter typed it into the proper file. "But Eagery's thing was a robot wolfman, as tall as me—me *now*, not in Hell. He could talk. He sounded like Eagery, actually." I turned to Frank. "The Happy Man's personality has a way of pervading his robots . . . "

Peter's cross-reference check flagged the wolfman entry,

38

and he punched up the reference. "In the south, Dad, remember? You met a wolfman, a real one, in the woods. You played Monopoly with him, then he turned into Colonel Eagery."

"Yeah, yeah. Never saw him again."

"Boy," said Frank, speaking for the first time since we'd punched up Hell. "You guys are thorough. What do you think the wolfman means?"

I froze up inside.

But before I could speak, Peter turned, twisted his mouth, and shook his head. "Hell doesn't *mean* anything," he said. "That's not the right approach." He'd heard the spiel a dozen times from me, and I guessed he'd sensed my tenderness on the issue; he was sticking up for his dad.

Then he surprised me by taking it further. "Hell is like an alternate world, like in *X-Men*. It's a real place, like here, only different. If you were going down the street and you met a wolfman, you wouldn't ask what it means. You'd run, or whatever."

Frank, who hadn't noticed my discomfort, winked at me and said, "Okay, Pete. I stand corrected."

Peter and I went back to our entry, more or less ignoring Frank. A few minutes later Maureen's car pulled up in the driveway. I tried not to let my sudden anxiety show, for the kid's sake.

"Tom."

She stood in Peter's doorway, still in her coat. When I looked up she didn't say anything more, just inclined her head in the direction of the bedroom. I gave Frank the seat beside Peter at the computer, and followed her.

"Look at you," she said when we were out of earshot.

"What?"

"When you're not drunk you're retreating into the

39

computer. It's just as bad, you know. Computer Hell. You've found a way to be there all the time, one way or another. You don't live here anymore."

"Maureen—"

"What's worse is the way you're taking him *with* you. Making him live in your Hell too. Making him think it's something great. When you're not here, he and his friends spend all day in front of that thing, living your Hell for you. Does it make you feel less lonely? Is that it?"

"I live here." I knew I had to keep my voice quiet and steady and fierce or she'd talk right over me, and soon we'd be shouting. I didn't want it to escalate. "Last thing I knew I lived here with *you*. Maybe that's not the way it is anymore. But I live here. Seems to me it's you who's got one foot out the door."

There was a moment of silence and then it hit me. Call me stupid, but it was the first time I felt the impact. Last night, making love, had been goodbye. The gulf between us now was enormous. Things weren't going to suddenly get better.

It would take a huge amount of very hard, very painful work to fix it, if it could be fixed at all.

"Do you ever think of the effect it has on *him?*" She was sticking to safe territory. I didn't blame her. She had a lot of it. "You and your goddamned *inner landscape*—"

She broke off, sobbing. It was as though she'd been saving those words, and their release had opened the floodgates. It also occurred to me that she was opting for tears so I wouldn't attack her, and I felt a little cheated.

Anyway, I took her in my arms. I'm not completely stupid.

"I don't want him to live like that," she said. Her fists balled against my chest for a moment, then her body went slack, and I had to hold her up while she cried. After a minute we sat on the edge of the bed.

"I don't know, Tom. I don't know what's happening."

"Well, neither do I." I felt suddenly exhausted and hollow. "It seems like the ball's in your court—"

I could feel her tensing up against my shoulder. So I dropped it.

I smelled onions frying in butter. I listened: Frank was cooking again, and explaining the recipe to Peter.

"It's not an inner landscape," I said quietly. "It's a place where I live half my life. I get to share that with my son—"

She pulled away from me and stood up, straightened her clothes. Then she went into the living room, without looking back.

16

I lay back on the bed, only meaning to buy some time. But I must have been depleted, morally and otherwise, and I fell asleep, and slept through dinner.

When I woke again the house was dark. Peter was in his room; I could see the glow of the night light in the hallway. Maureen was slipping into bed beside me.

When I reached for her she pushed me away.

I didn't make it into a big deal. I didn't feel particularly angry, not at the time. In a few minutes we were both asleep again.

17

When I woke again, it was to the sun streaming in across the bed, heating me to a sweat under the covers. It was Saturday; no work for me or Maureen, no school for Peter. But Maureen was gone. I didn't feel too good, and I lay there for a while just looking at the insides of my eyelids. There wasn't any noise in the apartment, and I suspected they'd all gone somewhere to get out from under the shadow of you-know-who.

I didn't let it bug me: I took a nice slow shower and went into the kitchen and made some coffee and toast.

But I was wrong. Peter was home. He wandered into the kitchen while I was cleaning up, and said, "Hey, Dad."

This time I could see he knew something was wrong. I didn't have what it took to keep it from him, and I guess he didn't have what it took to keep it from me, either.

"Hey, Pete," I said. "Where's your mom?"

"They went out shopping," he said. "Also to look at some place for Uncle Frank to live."

I nodded. "What you doing?"

"I don't know. Just some game stuff I got from Jeremy."

"It looks like a pretty nice day out there—"

"I know, I know. I heard it already, from Mom." He looked down at his feet.

There was a minute or two of silence while I finished clearing the table.

"I guess I should offer to 'throw the old pigskin around' or something," I said. "But the truth is I don't feel up to it right now."

The truth was my guts were churning. I couldn't focus on the kid. Seeing him left alone just made me think of Maureen and where she probably was right now. Frank was almost certainly playing the beard for her, and "shopping" by himself. If they came home with packages she'd have to unpack them to know what was in them.

"That's okay," he said seriously. "I don't think we have an old pigskin anyway."

I managed a smile.

"I'll be in my room, okay, Dad?"

"Okay, Peter."

Pretty soon I heard him tapping at his computer again. I sat and nursed the cold coffee and ran my thoughts through some pretty repetitive and unproductive loops. And then it hit me.

Just a twinge at first. But unmistakable.

I was on my way back to Hell.

I realized I'd felt inklings earlier that morning, in the shower, even in bed, and hadn't let myself notice. It was already pretty far along. I was probably an hour or so away from crossing over.

By this time I'd perfected a kind of emotional shorthand. I went through all the traditional stages in the space of a few seconds: denial, bargaining, fear, etc. But underlying them all, this time, was a dull, black rage.

I'd almost never had so short a time back. That hurt. The fact that I was crossing over while Maureen was holed up in her midday love nest hurt more. Unless she came back in the next hour, I wouldn't get in another word. I couldn't make up, couldn't plead, and I couldn't threaten, either, or issue an ultimatum. All the words I'd been rehearsing in my head flew right out the window. She would come home to find me a zombie again.

I felt my claim on her, and my claim on my own life—on Peter, the apartment, everything—slipping away. I had a sudden, desperate need to at least see Peter. I would cram two weeks' worth of unfinished business into the next hour. I got up and went into his room, my head whirling.

He turned from the computer when I appeared in his doorway. "Hey, Dad," he said. "Look at this. I had an idea about Hell."

I went and sat down beside him. I was afraid to open my mouth, afraid of what would or wouldn't come out. I

43

wanted to put on a big show of fatherly affection but I couldn't think of a damned thing to say.

Peter pretended not to notice. "Look." He'd punched up our entry for the starting point: the breakfast table, the horse, and the witch's house. "You get up from the table," he said. "You go off through the hedge in some direction, east, west, north, south. But there's a direction you never go in. It's so obvious. I can't believe we never thought of it."

It wasn't obvious to me, and I felt irritation. "Where? What direction?"

"*The witch's house.* You want breakfast, right? Why not just go in and get some? Why not find out what she's doing in there?"

The idea terrified me instantly. Me, a little boy, barging into the house of that beautiful, unapproachable woman. But Peter didn't know about the emotional content of Hell. I'd kept that from him. "It's an idea," I conceded. "Uh, yeah. It's an idea."

"It could be the key to the whole thing, Dad. Who knows. You've got to find out."

"The purloined letter," I said. "Something so obvious, just sitting right out there in plain sight, but nobody notices . . . " I was drifting off into talking to myself again. I couldn't stay focused on Peter. I was thinking about Maureen and her friend, and my thoughts were very, very murky.

"Will you try?" said Peter. "Will you check it out?"

"I might," I snapped, suddenly angry. It was as though he were taunting me. But of course he didn't know. I hadn't said anything.

He pretended he hadn't heard the tension in my voice, and went on, bright-eyed. "It could be nothing, really. Just another stupid dead end. Or the door is locked or something . . . "

"No, no," I said, wanting to reassure him now. "It's a good idea, Pete. An inspiration . . . "

We drifted off into a mutually embarrassed silence.

"Is Uncle Frank a lot like my grandfather?" asked Peter suddenly.

"Well, no. Not really. Why?"

"I dunno. He just seems so different from you. It's hard for me to see how you might be related. I can't imagine what your dad was like."

"Different how?"

"Oh, you know, Dad. You're so serious. Uncle Frank seems like he's almost younger than you."

"Younger?"

"He's just sillier, that's all. He says weird things. I can't really explain, but it's like he's some kind of cartoon character, or somebody you'd tell me about in a story. He reminds me of somebody from Hell, like the robot maker, or—"

That's where Peter stopped, because I hit him.

Hit him hard. Knocked him out of his chair and onto the floor.

My anger had been spiraling while he spoke. I thought about Frank out covering Maureen's ass, the two of them leaving the kid alone so she could squeeze in a quick lay, and that got me thinking about all the manipulative, unpleasant things Frank had done over the years. And now the kid was falling for it, falling for the image of the wacky, irresponsible, cartoon-character uncle who picked you up at school in the middle of the day, who seemed so much more charismatic than boring old Dad.

I remembered falling for it myself, and I wondered if my father ever felt anything like the jealousy I felt now.

Peter sat on the floor, whimpering. I held my hand up to

my face and looked at it, astonished. Then I walked out of the room. I couldn't face him. I couldn't think of what to say.

Besides, I was going to Hell.

I was glad. It was where I belonged.

18

I sat at the table a long time, watching the horse quiver and twitch as the flies crawled over his lips, watching the other children giggle and whisper and play with their silverware, listening to the sound of insects in the woods beyond the hedge, smelling the smoke that trailed out of the witch's chimney, quietly seething. I don't think I ever hated my Hell as badly as I did now. Now that my other life, my real life, had become a Hell too.

Eventually I got out of my seat. But I couldn't bring myself to run for the hedge to the north, or in any direction, for that matter. I stood on the grass beside my chair, paralyzed by Peter's suggestion. After a minute or so I took a first, tentative step across the grass, toward the witch's hut. It seemed like a mile to the cobblestone steps at the door. I tried the handle; it turned easily. The room was dark. I stepped inside.

The Happy Man was turned away from me, facing the table, his pants down around his ankles, his pale, hairy buttocks squeezed together. Splayed out on the table, her bare legs in the air, was the witch. The Happy Man had one hand over her mouth, the other on her breasts.

"Oh, shit," he said when he heard me come in. He stopped thrusting and hurriedly pulled up his pants. "What are you doing in here?" He turned away, left the witch scrambling to cover herself on the table. Despite my astonishment at finding Eagery in the hut, I managed to ogle her for a moment. She was beautiful.

"Breakfast," I got out. "I wanted breakfast."

"Oh, yeah?" The Happy Man didn't sound playful. He was advancing on me fast. I tried to turn and leave, but he grabbed me and pinned me against the wall. "Breakfast is served," he said. He lifted me by my belt and took me to the stove. I could feel its heat as I dangled there. He opened the door with his free hand. Inside there was a pie baking; it smelled wonderful. The breakfast we'd always hoped for. Eagery dropped me onto the open door.

My hands and knees immediately burned. I heard myself pleading, but The Happy Man didn't pay any attention; he began pushing the door closed, wedging me into the hot oven with the pie, battering at my dangling arms and legs until I pulled them in, then slamming the door closed and leaning on it with his full weight.

I fell into the pie, and burning sugar stuck to my back. I think I screamed. Eagery kicked at the oven, jolting it off the floor, until I was silent. Eventually I died.

Died back into my own life, of course. Peter was right. He'd discovered a shortcut.

Lucky me.

19

I came back in the apartment this time, sitting alone in the living room, watching television. That's how I spend a lot of my zombie hours, according to Maureen. It was midday, and I suspected I hadn't been away long at all. I checked my watch. Sure enough, less than twenty-four hours had passed. It was the second day of the weekend; my shortest stay in Hell ever, by several days.

I turned off the television and went into the kitchen to make myself some coffee. The house was empty. The day was pretty bright, and I suspected they'd gone out for a picnic or something up at the park. I had a few hours alone with my thoughts.

Still, it wasn't until I heard their car in the driveway that I had my big idea.

I had the tube on again. That was part of it. It had something to do with not wanting to face them, too. Not knowing what to say to Maureen, or Peter. When I heard the car pull up I felt my tongue go numb in my mouth.

By the time Maureen got her key in the door it was a fully hatched plan. I stared at the television as they came in, keeping my breath steady, trying not to meet their eyes. There was a moment of silence as Maureen checked me out and determined that I was still away, in Hell.

Then the conversation picked up again, like I wasn't even there.

"—what's he watching?"

"That horrible cop thing. Peter, for God's sake, turn it down. I don't want to listen to that. Or change the channel—" To Frank: "He won't notice. If he doesn't like it, he'll just get up and go away. But he never does. I've seen him sit through hours and hours of Peter's horror things . . . "

I would have enjoyed proving her wrong, but I didn't want to risk anything that would blow my cover. So I sat there while Peter flipped the dial, settling eventually on the news.

The lead story was a minor quake in L.A., and like all good Californians they took the bait, crowded around me on the couch for a look at the damage: a couple of tilted cars on a patch of split pavement, a grandmother face-down on her lawn, pet dog sniffing at her displaced wig. Maureen and Frank sat to my left, and Peter pushed up close to me at

my right. It was our first physical contact in a long time—
unless you counted the punch.

But Peter didn't sit still for very long. He squirmed in his
seat until Maureen noticed.

"Mom?" he said. When he leaned forward I saw the big
purple bruise I'd left on the side of his face.

"What?"

He held his nose and made a face. "I think Dad needs a
shower."

20

The quality of their disregard was terrifying. I wasn't, as I'd
flattered myself by imagining, a monster in their midst, a
constant reminder of a better life that had eluded them.
They weren't somber or mournful at all. They *coped*. I was a
combination of a big, stupid pet and an awkward,
unplugged appliance too big for the closet. I was in the way.
It was too soon for them to begin hoping—or dreading—
that I'd come back, and in the meantime I was a hungry,
smelly nuisance.

When Maureen leaned in close and suggested I go clean
myself up, I knew to agree politely and follow the suggestion. I welcomed the chance to get away from them and
reconnoiter, anyway.

When I emerged from my shower they were already at
the table eating. I suppose I shouldn't have expected an invi-
tation. They'd set a place for me, and I went and sat in it,
and ate, quietly, and listened while they talked.

The subject of Peter's "injury" came up only once, and
then just barely. I gathered that Frank and Maureen had
decided to suppress any discussion, to play it down, and
hope that Peter was still young enough that he would just

plain forget. Find some childlike inner resource for blurring experience into fantasy.

Maybe they would confront me later, when I came back, with Peter out at a friend's house. But the subject was obviously taboo right now.

The discussion mostly centered on Frank's plans. The apartment he was looking at, and some second thoughts he seemed to be having about settling in this area. I sensed an undercurrent, between him and Maureen, of what wasn't being discussed: Frank's trouble. The phone calls he was avoiding. Yet more stuff for Peter not to hear. I wondered, though, knowing Peter's smarts, how much he was picking up anyway.

I was dying for a drink. I tried not to let it show on my face.

After the meal Frank pleaded exhaustion and went into the guest room, and Maureen read a book on the bed. I set up in front of the television and tried not to think about what I was doing or why I was doing it. I walked through the apartment a couple of times on my way to the bathroom, and when I passed Peter's door he looked up from his computer, and I had to struggle not to meet his eye. He would have admired my ruse, and I would have liked to let him in on it, but that wasn't possible. So I stalked past his room like a zombie, and he turned back to his homework. I spent most of the evening on the couch, slogging through prime time. After Maureen tucked Peter into bed I followed her into the bedroom.

She made the phone call about five minutes after she turned off the lights.

"Philip?" she whispered.

A pause.

"Can you talk? I couldn't sleep." Pause. "No, he's right

here in bed with me. Of course he can't hear. I mean it doesn't matter, even if he can. No. No. It's not that." She sighed. "I just miss you."

I guess he talked a bit.

"You do?" she said, her voice half-melted. I hadn't heard her that way in a while. "Philip. Yes, I know. But it's not that easy. You know. Yes. I wish I could."

They went on like that. Her voice was quiet enough that Peter and Frank wouldn't hear, but in the darkened bedroom it was like a stage play. I could almost make out her boyfriend's tinny replies over the phone.

Then she giggled and said, "I'm touching myself too."

Thank God it was dark. My face must have been crimson. I felt the room whirling like a centrifuge, the bed at the center. I weighed a thousand or a million pounds and I was crushed into my place there on the bed beside Maureen by the pressure of gravity. I couldn't move. I felt my blood pounding in my wrists and temples.

Why was I there? What was I trying to prove?

I knew, dimly, that I'd had some reason for the deception, that some part of me had insisted that there was something I could learn, something vital.

It couldn't have been this, though. I didn't need this.

So what was I after? What—

I sat bolt upright in the bed, dislodging the covers.

"Huh?" said Maureen. "Nothing, nothing. Listen, I have to go, I'll call you back." She hung up and turned on the light. I turned and looked at her in shock. She opened her mouth to scream, and somehow I got my hand over her mouth first. I wrestled her down against the bed, pushed her face into the pillow, twisted her arm behind her back, put my weight on her.

I could hear her yelling my name into the pillow, wetly. Her ears were bright red.

I tightened my grip on her arm. "Shhh," I said, close to her ear. "No noise. No noise." I listened at the hall, alert now, panicked. I had to convince her. "No noise."

"You're dead," she hissed when I let her up for air. "All I have to do is report you. You're dead." Her eyes were slits.

"Shhh." I let her go, forgot her. Focused on the hall.

There wasn't any light. Peter's night light was out, or his door was closed.

Impossible. Peter wouldn't permit it.

Someone was in the house. Frank's pals.

I slid into my pants, silently. I was operating with my Hell-reflexes now, and they were good. There wasn't going to be any hostage. I would make sure of that. I would have complete surprise.

I turned back to Maureen. "Call your pal," I whispered. "Keep it quiet. Have him bring in the cops, but quiet, and slow." She looked at me, stunned out of her outrage. "I'm serious. Call him. And stay in here. Whatever happens."

I didn't leave her time for questions. In my pants and bare feet I crept out into the hall and made my way to Peter's door.

Inside I heard him whimpering softly, as if through a gag.

I burst in.

Peter was spread-eagled on his bed, bound with neckties. His pajamas were in shreds around his ankles. Frank, who wasn't wearing anything at all, was kneeling on the side of the bed, as if praying over Peter's helpless body. One hand was resting lightly on Peter's stomach. In the other hand he held his own penis. His pubic hair was white. He looked up at me and his eyes widened for a moment, then fell. And then he grinned. His hands stayed where they were.

I picked up Peter's keyboard and smashed it against Frank's white skull. He straightened up and stopped grinning, and reached back to feel his head.

"Tommy," he said, his voice soft, almost beguiling.

I drew the keyboard back like a baseball bat and hit him again. This time I drew blood. I didn't stop hitting him until he fell back against the floor, his mouth open, his eyes full of tears, his erection wilting.

Peter watched the whole thing from the bed, his mouth gagged, his eyes wide. When I dropped the keyboard and looked up, he met my eyes, for a minute. Then I looked away. I found his floppy disks for Hell, the main disk and the backup, and I tore them in half and tossed them onto the floor, beside Frank.

Peter didn't get untied until the police showed up. Maureen was hiding in her room and I, try as I might, just couldn't bring myself to *touch* him.

21

I live alone now. The settlement went like this: I see Peter every other weekend—if I happen to be back from Hell, that is—and only in the company of his mother. And I don't go anywhere near the house.

Yes, Uncle Frank was Colonel Eagery, aka The Happy Man. He'd molested me as a boy, right in our house, while my father was away, and with my mother in the kitchen making breakfast. I remember it all now.

And yes, I killed him.

Needless to say, there wasn't any Mob on his trail. The call he'd been dreading was the Baltimore police. He was on the run from a molestation offense.

Like I said, I live alone. It's a pretty nice place, and a lot closer to the station. There's a pretty nice bar around the corner. Different crowd every night.

Yes, I still go to Hell, but it's different now. There isn't any horse, or witch, or Happy Man. There isn't even a forest.

When I go to Hell now it's like this:

I'm back in the house with Maureen and Peter. I live with them again. But I'm unable to speak, or reach out to them: I'm a zombie. I start by sitting in front of the television, flipping channels, and then eventually I wander around the apartment, brushing past Maureen, but never able to speak to her, never able to take her hand or hold her or lead her into the bedroom. After a while I go and stand in the doorway of Peter's room. He turns and looks up at me, but I look away, afraid to meet his eye. I pretend to look the other way, and he goes back to his computer.

And that's it. I spend the rest of the time standing in his doorway, looking over his shoulder at the computer screen.

Watching him play my Hell.

Access Fantasy

There was a start-up about a half-mile ahead the day before, a fever of distant engines and horns honking as others signalled their excitement—a chance to move!—and so he'd spent the day jammed behind the wheel, living in his Apartment On Tape, waiting for that chance, listening under the drone of distant helicopters to hear the start-up make its way downtown. But the wave of revving engines stalled before reaching his street. He never even saw a car move, just heard them. In fact he couldn't remember seeing a car move recently. Perhaps the start-up was only a panic begun by someone warming their motor, reviving their battery. That night he'd dreamed another start-up, or perhaps it was real, a far-off flare that died before he'd even ground the sleep out of his eyes, though in the rustle of his waking thoughts it was a perfect thing, coordinated, a dance of cars shifting through the free-flowing streets. Dream or not, either way, didn't matter. He fell back asleep. What woke him in the morning was the family in the Pacer up ahead cooking breakfast. They had a stove on the roof of their car and the dad was grilling something they'd bought from the flatbed shepherd two blocks away, a sheepsteak or something. It smelled good. Everything about the family in the Pacer made him too conscious of his wants. The family's daughter—she was beautiful—had been working as Advertising, pushing up against and through the One-Way Permeable Barrier on behalf of some vast faceless corporation. That being the only way through the One-Way Permeable Barrier, of course. So the family, her Ma and Pa, were flush, had dough, and vendors knew to seek them out, hawking groceries. Whereas checking his pockets he didn't have more than a couple of dollars. There was a coffee-and-donuts man threading his way through the traffic even now but coffee was beyond his means. He needed money. Rumors had it Welfare Helicopters had been sighted south of East One Thousand, One Hundred and Ninety-Fourth Street, and a lot of people had left their cars, drifted down that way, looking for easy cash. Which was one reason the start-up died, it occurred to him—too many empty cars. Along with the cars that wouldn't start anymore, like the old lady in the Impala beside him, the dodderer. She'd given up, spent most days dozing in the back seat. Her nephew from a few blocks away came over and tinkered with her engine now and again but it wasn't helping. It just meant the nephew wasn't at his wheel for the start-up, another dead spot, another reason not to bother waiting to move. Probably he thought now he should have walked downtown himself in search of welfare money drifting down from the sky. The state helicopters weren't coming around this neighborhood much lately. Alas. The air was crowded with commercial hovercraft instead, recruiters, Advertising robots rounding up the girl from the Pacer and others like her, off to the world on the other side of the One-Way Permeable Barrier, however briefly. The world of Apartments, real ones. Though it was morning he went back to his latest Apartment On Tape, which was a four bedroom two bath co-op on East One Thousand, Two Hundred and Fifteenth Street, just a few blocks away but another world of course, remote from his life on the street, sealed off from it by the One-Way Permeable Barrier. He preferred the early part of the tape, before any of the furnishings arrived, so he rewound to that part and put the tape on slow and lived in the rooms as hard as he could, ignoring the glare of sun through his windshield that dulled his view of the dashboard television, ignoring the activities of the family in the Pacer up ahead as they clambered in and out of the hatchback, ignoring the clamor of his own pangs. The realtor's voice was annoying, it was a squawking, parroty voice so he kept the volume down as always and lived in the rooms silently, letting his mind sweep in and haunt the empty spaces, the rooms unfolding in slow motion for the realtor's camera. While the camera lingered in the bathroom he felt under his seat for his bottle and unzipped and peed, timed so it matched to the close-up of the automatic flushing of the toilet on his television. Then the camera and his attention wandered out into the hall. That's when he noticed it, the shadow. Just for a moment. He rewound to see it again. On the far wall of the hallway, framed perfectly for an instant in the lens the silhouette of a struggle, a man with his hands on the neck of another, smaller. A woman. Shaking her by the neck for that instant, before the image vanished. Like a pantomime of murder, a Punch-and-Judy show hidden in the Apartment On Tape. But real, it had to be real. Why hadn't he noticed before? He'd watched this tape dozens of times. He rewound again. Just barely, but still. Unmistakable, however brief. The savagery of it was awful. If only he could watch it frame by frame—slow motion was disastrously fast now. Who was the killer? The landlord? The realtor? Why? Was the victim the previous tenant? Questions, he had questions. He felt himself begin to buzz with them, come alive. Slow motion didn't seem particularly

57

slow precisely because his attention had quickened. Yes, a job of detection was just what he needed to roust himself out of the current slump, burn off the torpor of too many days locked in the jam at the same damn intersection—why hadn't he gone Downtown at that last turnoff, months ago? Well, anyway. He watched it again, memorized the shadow, the silhouette, imagined blurred features in the slurry of video fuzz, memorized the features, what the hell. Like a police sketch, work from his own prescient hallucinations. Again. It grew sharper every time. He'd scrape a hole in this patch of tape, he knew, if he rewound too many times. Better to have the tape, the evidence, all there was at this point. He popped the video, threw it in a satchel with notebook, eyeglasses. Extra socks. Outside, locked the car, tipped an imaginary hat at the old lady, headed east by foot on West One Thousand, Two Hundred and Eighth Street. He had to duck uptown two blocks to avoid a flotilla of Sanitation hovertrucks spraying foamy water to wash cars sealed up tight against this artificial rain but also soaking poor jerks asleep, drenching interiors, the rotted upholstery and split spongy dashboards, extinguishing rooftop bonfires, destroying box gardens, soap bubbles poisoning the feeble sprouts. Children screamed and giggled, the streets ran with water, sluicing shit here and there into drains, more often along under the tires to the unfortunate neighboring blocks, everyone moaning and lifting their feet clear. Just moving it around, that's all. Around the next corner he ran into a crowd gathered staring at a couple of young teenage girls from inside, from the apartments, the other side of the Barrier. They'd come out of the apartment building on rollerblades to sightsee, to slum on the streets. Sealed in a murky bubble of One-Way Permeable Barrier they were like apparitions, dim ghosts, though you could hear them giggle as they skated through the hushed, reverent crowd. Like a sighting of gods, these teenage girls from inside. No one bothered to spare-change them or bother them in any way because of the Barrier. The girls of course were oblivious behind their twilight veil, like night things come into the day, though for them probably it was the people in cars and around the cars that appeared dim, unreachable. He shouldered his way through the dumbstruck crowd and once past this obstacle he found his man, locked into traffic like all the rest, right where he'd last seen him. The Apartments On Tape dealer, his connection, sunbathing in a deck chair on the roof of his Sentra, eating a sandwich. The backseat was stacked with realtor's tapes apartment porn and on the passenger seat two video decks for dubbing. His car in a sliver of morning sun that shone across the middle of the block, benefit of a chink in the canyon of towers that surrounded them. The dealer's neighbors were on their car roofs as well, stretching in the sun, drying clothes. "Hello there, remember me? That looks good what you're eating, anyway, I want to talk to you about this tape." "No refunds," said the dealer, not even looking down. "No, that's not it, I saw something, can we watch it together?" "No need since there's no refunds and I'm hardly interested—" "Listen, this is a police matter, I think—" "You're police then, is that what you're saying?" still not looking down. "No no, I fancy myself a private detective, though not to say I work outside the law, more adjacent, then turn it over to them if it serves justice, there's so often corruption—" "So turn it over," the dealer said. "Well if you could just have a look I'd value your opinion. Sort of pick your brain," thinking flattery or threats, should have chosen one approach with this guy, stuck with it. The dealer said, "Sorry, day off," still not turning his head, chewing off another corner of sandwich.

Something from inside the sandwich fell, a chunk of something, fish maybe, onto the roof of the car. "The thing is I think I saw a murder, on the tape, in the apartment." "That's highly unlikely." "I know, but that's what I saw." "Murder, huh?" The dealer didn't sound at all impressed. "Bloody body parts, that sort of thing?" "No, don't be absurd, just a shadow, just a trace." "Hmmm." "You never would have noticed in passing. Hey, come to think of it, you don't have an extra sandwich do you?" "No, I don't. So would you describe this shadow as sort of a flicker then, like a malfunction?" "No, absolutely not. It's part of the tape." "Not your monitor on the fritz?" "No," he was getting angry now, "a person, a shadow strangling another shadow." The chunk of sandwich filling on the car roof was sizzling slightly, changing color already in the sun. The dealer said, "Shadows, hmmm. Probably a gimmick, subliminal special effects or something." "What? What reason would a realtor have for adding special effects for God's sake to an apartment tape?" "Maybe they think it adds some kind of allure, some thrill of menace that makes their apartments stand out from the crowd." "I doubt very much—" "Maybe they've become aware of the black market in tapes lately, that's the word on the street in fact, and so they're trying to send a little message. They don't like us ogling their apartments, even vicariously." "You can't ogle vicariously, I think. Sounds wrong. Anyway, that's the most ridiculous thing I've ever—" "Or maybe I'm in on it, maybe I'm the killer, have you considered that?" "Now you're making fun of me." "Why? If you can solve crimes on the other side of the Barrier why can't I commit them?" The dealer laughed, hyena-like. "Now seriously," he continued, "if you want to exchange for one without a murder I'll give you a credit towards the next, half what you paid—" "No thanks. I'll hold onto it." Discouraged, hungry, but he couldn't really bother being angry. What help did he expect from the dealer anyway? This was a larger matter, above the head of a mere middleman. "Good luck, Sherlock," the dealer was saying. "Spread word freely, by the way, don't hold back. Can't hurt my sales any. People like murder, only it might be good if there was skin instead of only shadow, a tit say." "Yes, very good then, appreciate your help. Carry on." The dealer saluted. He saluted back, started off through the traffic, stomach growling, ignoring it, intent. A killer was at large. Weaving past kids terrorizing an entire block of cars with an elaborate tag game, cornering around the newly washed neighborhood now wringing itself out, muddy streams between the cars and crying babies ignoring vendors with items he couldn't afford and a flatbed farmer offering live kittens for pets or food and a pathetic miniature start-up, three cars idiotically nosing rocking jerking back and forth trying to rearrange themselves pointlessly, one of them now sideways wheels on the curb and nobody else even taking the bait he made his way back to his car and key in the lock noticed the girl from the Pacer standing in her red dress on the hood of the car gazing skyward, waiting for the Advertising people to take her away. Looking just incidentally like a million bucks. Her kid brother was away, maybe part of the gang playing tag, and her parents were inside the car doing housework dad scraping the grill out the window mom airing clothes repacking bundles so he went over, suddenly inspired. "Margaret, isn't it?" She nodded, smiled. "Yes, good, well you remember me from next door, I'm looking for a day or two's work and do you think they'll take me along?" She said, "You never know, they just take you or they don't." Smiling graciously even if a little confused, so long neighbors and they'd never spoken. "But you always—"

he began pointing out. She said, "Oh once they've started taking you then—" Awkwardly, they were both awkward for a moment not saying what they both knew or at least he did, that she was an attractive young girl and likely that made a huge difference in whether they wanted you. "Well you wouldn't mind if I tried?" he said and she said "No, no," relieved almost, then added "I can point you out, I can suggest to them—" Now he was embarrassed and said hurriedly, "That's so good of you, thanks, and where should I wait, not here with you at your folks' car, I guess—" "Why not, climb up." Dad looked out the door up at them and she waved him off, "It's okay, you know him from next door he's going to work, we're going to try to get him a job Advertising." "Okay, sweetheart just checking on you." Then she grabbed his arm, said, "Look." The Advertising hovercraft she'd been watching for landed on the curb a half-block ahead, near the giant hideous sculpture at an office building main entrance, lately sealed. Dad said, "Get going you guys, and good luck," and she said, "C'mon." Such neighborliness was a surprise since he'd always felt shut out by the family in the Pacer but obviously it was in his head. And Margaret, a cloud of good feeling seemed to cover her. No wonder they wanted her for Advertising. "Hurry," she said and took his hand and they hopped down and pushed their way around the cars and through the chaos of children and barking dogs and vendors trying to work the crowd of wannabees these landings always provoked, to join the confused throng at the entrance. He held onto his satchel with the video and his socks making sure it didn't get picked in this crowd. She bounced there trying to make herself visible until one of the two robots at the door noticed her and pointed. They stepped up. "Inside," said the robot. They were ugly little robots with their brain-cases undisguised and terrible attitudes. He disliked them instantly. "I brought someone new," she said, pulling him by the hand, thrusting him into view. "Yes, sir, I'd like to enlist—" he started, grinning madly, wanting to make a good impression. The robot looked him over and made its rapid-fire assessment, nodded. "Get inside," it said. "Lucky," she whispered, and they stepped into the hovercraft. Four others were there, two men, two women, all young. And another woman stumbled in behind them, and the door sealed, and they were off. Nasty little robots scurrying into the cockpit, making things ready. "Now what?" he said and she put her finger to her lips and shushed him, but sweetly, leaning into him as if to say they were in this together. He wanted to tell her what he was after but the robots might hear. Would they care? Yes, no, he couldn't know. Such ugly, fascistic little robots. Nazi robots, that's what they were. He hated placing himself in their hands. But once he was Advertising he would be through the barrier, he'd be able to investigate. Probably he should keep his assignment to himself, though. He didn't want to get her into trouble. The hovercraft shuddered, groaned, then lifted and through the window he could see the cars growing smaller, his neighborhood, his life, the way the traffic was so bad for hundreds of miles of street and why did he think a start-up would change anything? Was there a place where cars really drove anymore? Well, anyway. The robots were coming around with the Advertising Patches and everyone leaned their heads forward obediently, no first-timers like himself apparently. He did the same. A robot fastened a patch behind his right ear, a moment of stinging skin, nothing more. Hard to believe the patch was enough to interfere with the function of the One-Way Permeable Barrier, that he would now be vivid and tangible and effective to those on the other side. "I don't feel any different," he whispered. "You won't," she said. "Not until there's people. Then you'll be compelled to Advertise. You won't be able to help it." "For what, though?" "You never know, coffee, diamonds, condoms, vacations, you just never know." "Where—" "They'll drop us off at the Undermall, then we're on our own." "Will we be able to stick together?" The question was out before he could wonder if it was presuming too much, but she said, "Sure, as long as our products aren't too incompatible, but we'll know soon. Anyway, just follow me." She really had a warmth, a glow. Incompatible products? Well, he'd find out what that meant. The hovercraft bumped down on the roof of a building, and with grim efficiency the ugly Nazi robots had the door open and were marching the conscripts out to a rooftop elevator. He wanted to reach out and smack their little exposed-braincase heads together. But he had to keep his cool, stay undercover. He trotted across the roof towards the elevator after her, between the rows of officious gesticulating robots, like they were going to a concentration camp. The last robot at the door of the elevator handed them each an envelope before they stepped in. He took his and moved into the corner with Margaret, they were really packing them in but he couldn't complain actually being jostled with her and she didn't seem to be trying to avoid it. He poked into the envelope. It was full of bills, singles mostly. The money was tattered and filthy, bills that had been taken out of circulation on the other side of the Barrier. Garbage money, that's what it was. The others had already pocketed theirs, business as usual apparently. "Why do they pay us now?" he whispered. She said "We just find our way out at the end, when the patch runs out, so this way they don't have to deal with us again," and he said "What if we just took off with

64

the money?" "You could I guess, but I've never seen anyone do it since you'd never get to come back and anyway the patch makes you really want to Advertise, you'll see." Her voice was reassuring, like she really wanted him not to worry and he felt rotten not telling her about his investigation, his agenda. He put the envelope into his satchel with tape and socks. The elevator sealed and whooshed them down through the building, into the Undermall, then the doors opened and they unpacked from the elevator, spewed out into a gigantic lobby, all glass and polished steel with music playing softly and escalators going down and up in every direction, escalators with steps of burnished wood that looked good enough to eat, looked like roast chicken. He was still so hungry. Margaret took his hand again. "Let's go," she said. As the others dispersed she led him towards one of the escalators and they descended. The corridor below branched to shops with recessed entrances, windows dark and smoky, quiet pulsing music fading from each door, also food smells here and there causing his saliva to flow, and holographic signs angling into view as they passed: FERN SLAW, ROETHKE AND SONS, HOLLOW APPEAL, BROKEN SMUDGED ALPHABET, BURGER KING, PLASTIC DEVILS, OSTRICH LAKE, SMARTINGALE'S, RED HARVEST, CATCH OF THE DAY, MUTUAL OF FOMALHAUT, THNEEDS, et cetera. She led him on, confidently, obviously at home. Why not, this was what she did with her days. Then without warning, a couple appeared from around a corner, and he felt himself begin to Advertise. "How do you do today?" he said, sidling up to the gentleman of the couple, even as he saw Margaret begin to do the same thing to the lady. The gentleman nodded at him, walked on. But met his eye. He was tangible, he could be heard. It was a shock. "Thirsty?" he heard himself say. "How long's it been since you had a nice refreshing beer?"

"Don't like beer," said the gentleman. "Can't say why, just never have." "Then you've obviously never tried a Very Old Money Lager," he heard himself say, still astonished. The Barrier was pierced and he was conversing, he was perceptible. He'd be able to conduct interrogations, be able to search out clues. Meanwhile he heard Margaret saying "Don't demean your signature with a second-rate writing implement. Once you've tried the Eiger fountain pen you'll never want to go back to those hen-like scratchings and scrawlings," and the woman seemed interested and so Margaret went on "our Empyrean Sterling Silver Collection features one-of-a-kind hand-etched casings—" In fact the man seemed captivated too he turned ignoring the beer pitch and gave Margaret his attention. "Our brewers hand-pick the hops and malt," he was unable to stop though he'd obviously lost his mark, "and every single batch of fire-brewed Very Old Money Lager is individually tasted—" Following the couple through the corridor they bumped into another Advertising woman who'd been on the hovercraft, and she began singing, "Vis-it-the *moon*, it's nev-er too *soon*," dancing sinuously and batting her eyes, distracting them all from fountain pens and beer for the moment and then the five of them swept into the larger space of the Undermall and suddenly there were dozens of people who needed to be told about the beer, "Thirsty? Hello, hi there, thirsty? Excuse me, thirsty? Yes? Craving satisfaction, sparkle, bite? No? Yes? Have you tried Very Old Money? What makes it different, you ask—oh, hello, thirsty?" and also dozens of people working as Advertising, a gabble of pitches—stern, admonitory: "Have you considered the perils of being without success insurance?" flippant, arbitrary: "You never know you're out with the Black Underwear Crowd, not until you get one of them home!" jingly, singsong: "We've

66

got children, we've all got children, you can have children too—" and as they scattered and darted along the endless marble floors of the Undermall he was afraid he'd lose her, but there was Margaret, earnestly discussing pens with a thoughtful older couple and he struggled over towards her, hawking beer—"Thirsty? Oof, sorry, uh, thirsty?" The crowd thinned as customers ducked into shops and stole away down corridors back to their apartments, bullied by the slew of Advertising except for the few like this older couple who seemed gratified by the attention, he actually had to wait as they listened and took down some information from her about the Eiger fountain pen while he stood far enough away to keep from barking at them about the beer. Then once the older couple wandered off he took Margaret's hand this time, why not, she'd done it, and drew her down a corridor away from the crowds, hoping to keep from engaging with any more customers, and also in the right direction if he had his bearings. He thought he did. He led her into the shadow of a doorway, a shop called FINGER-TOES that wasn't doing much business. "Listen, I've got to tell you something, I haven't been completely truthful, I mean, I haven't lied, but there's something—" She looked at him, hopeful, confused, but generous in her interpretation, he could tell, what a pure and sweet disposition, maybe her dad wasn't such a bad guy after all if he'd raised a plum like this. "I'm a detective, I mean, what does that mean, really, but the thing is there's been a murder and I'm trying to look into it—" and then he plunged in and told all, the Apartment On Tape, pulling it out of his satchel to show her, the shadow, the strangling, his conversation with the dealer and then his brainstorm to slip inside the citadel, slip past the One-Way Permeable Barrier that would of course have kept his questions or accusations from even being audible to those on this side, and so he'd manipulated her generosity to get aboard the hovercraft. "Forgive me," he said. Her eyes widened, her voice grew hushed, reverent. "Of course, but what do you want to do? Find the police?" "You're not angry at me?" "No, no. It's a brave thing you're doing." "Thank you." They drew closer. He could almost kiss her, just in happiness, solidarity, no further meaning or if there was it was just on top of the powerful solidarity feeling, just an extra, a windfall. "But what do you think is best, the police?" she whispered. "No, I have in mind a visit to the apartment, we're only a couple of blocks away, in this direction I believe, but do you think we can get upstairs?" They fell silent then because a man swerved out of FINGERTOES with a little paper tray of greasy fried things, looked like fingers or toes in fact and smelled terrific, he couldn't believe how hungry he was. "Thirsty?" he said hopelessly and the man popping one into his mouth said, "You called it brother, I'm dying for a beer." "Why just any beer when you could enjoy a Very Old Money—" and he had to go on about it, being driven nuts by the smell, while Margaret waited. The moment the grease-eater realized they were Advertising and broke free, towards the open spaces of the Undermall he and Margaret broke in the other direction, down the corridor. "This way," said Margaret, turning them towards the elevator, "the next level down you can go for blocks, it's the way out eventually too." "Yes, but can we get back upstairs?" "The elevators work for us until the patches run out, I think," and so they went down below the Undermall to the underground corridors, long echoey halls of tile, not so glamorous as upstairs, not nice at all really, the lengths apartment people went to, never to have to step out onto the street and see car people being really appalling sometimes. The tunnels were marked with street signs, names of other

Undermalls, here and there an exit. They had to Advertise only once before reaching East One Thousand, Two Hundred and Fifteenth Street, to a group of teenage boys smoking a joint in the corridor who laughed and asked Margaret questions she couldn't answer like are they mightier or less mighty than the sword and do they work for pigs. They ran into another person Advertising, a man moving furtively who when he recognized Margaret was plainly relieved. "He's got a girlfriend," she explained, somewhat enigmatically. So those Advertising could, did—what? Interact. But caught up in the chase now, he didn't ask more, just counted the blocks, feeling the thrill of approaching his Apartment On Tape's real address. They went up in the elevator, which was lavish again, wood panelled and perfumed and mirrored and musical. An expensive building. Apartment 16D so he pressed the button for the sixteenth floor, holding his breath, hardly believing it when they rose above the public floors. But they did. He gripped her hand. The elevator stopped on the sixth floor and a robot got on. Another of the creepily efficient braincase-showing kind. At first the robot ignored them but then on the fifteenth floor a woman got on and Margaret said, "The most personal thing about you is your signature, don't you think?" and he said, "Thirsty?" and the robot turned and stared up at them. The doors closed and they rode up to the sixteenth floor, and the three of them got out, he and Margaret and the robot, leaving the woman behind. The hallway was splendid with plush carpeting and brass light fixtures, empty apart from the three of them. "What are you doing up here?" said the robot. "And what's in that bag?" Clutching his satchel he said, "Nothing, just my stuff." "Why is it any of your business?" said Margaret, surprisingly defiant. "We've been asked to give an extended presentation at a customer's private home," he

69

said, wanting quickly to cover Margaret's outburst, give the robot something else to focus on. "Then I'll escort you," said the robot. "You really don't have to do that," he said, and Margaret said, bizarrely, "Don't come along and screw up our pitch, we'll sue you." Learning of the investigation had an odd effect on her, always a risk working with amateurs he supposed. But also it was these robots, the way they were designed with rotten personalities or no personalities they really aroused revulsion in people, it was an instinctual thing and not just him, he noted with satisfaction. He squeezed her hand and said, "Our sponsors would be displeased, it's true." "This matter requires clearance," said the robot, trying to get in front of them as they walked, and they had to skip to stay ahead of it. "Please stand to one side and wait for clearance," but they kept going down the carpeted hallway, his fingers crossed that it was the right direction for 16D. "Halt," said the robot, a flashing red light on its forehead beginning to blink neurotically and then they were at the door, and he rapped with his knuckles, thinking, hardly going incognito here, but better learn what we can. "Stand to one side," said the robot again. "Shut up," said Margaret. As the robot clamped a steely hand on each of their arms, jerking them back away from the door, its treads grinding on the carpet for traction, probably leaving ugly marks too, the door swung open. "Hello?" The man in the doorway was unshaven and slack-haired wearing a robe and blinking at them as though he'd only turned on his light to answer the door. "They claim to have an appointment with you sir," said the robot. The man only stood and stared. "It's very important, we have to talk to you urgently," he said, trying to pull free of the robot's chilly grip, then added, regretfully, "about beer." He felt a swoon at looking through the doorway, realizing he was seeing into his Apartment On Tape, the rooms etched into his dreamy brain now before him. He tried to see more but the light was gloomy. "—and fountain pens," said Margaret, obviously trying to hold herself back but compelled to chip something. "I apologize sir I tried to detain them to obtain clearance—" said the robot. *Detain, obtain*, what rotten syntax, he thought, the people who program these robots certainly aren't poets. The man just stood and blinked and looked them over, the three of them struggling subtly, he and Margaret trying to pull free of the robot, which was still blinking red and grinding at the carpet. "Cooperate," squawked the robot. The man in the robe squinted at them, finally smiled. "Please," said Margaret. "Fountain pens, eh?" the man in the robe said at last. "Yes," said Margaret desperately, and he heard himself add "And beer—" "Yes, of course," mumbled the man in the robe. "How silly of me. Come in." "Sir, for your safety—" "They're fine," said the man to the robot. "I'm expecting them. Let them in." The robot released its grip. The man in the robe turned and shuffled inside. They followed him, all three of them, into poorly-lit rooms disastrously heaped with newspapers, clothes, soiled dishes, empty and half-empty takeout packages, but still unmistakably the rooms from his tape, every turn of his head recalling some camera movement and there sure enough was the wall that had held the shadow, the momentary stain of murder. The man in the robe turned and said to the robot, "Please wait outside." "But surely I should chaperone, sir—" "No, that's fine, just outside the door, I'll call you in if I need you. Close it on your way out, thanks." Watching the robot slink back out he couldn't help but feel a little thrill of vindication. The man in the robe continued into the kitchen, and gesturing at the table said, "Please, sit, sorry for the mess. Did you say you'd like a beer?" "Well, uh, no, that wasn't exactly—if you drink beer you ought to make it a Very Old Money Lager for full satisfaction—but I've got something else to discuss while you enjoy your delicious, oh, damn it—" "Relax, have a seat. Can I get you something else?" "Food," he blurted. "Which always goes best with a Very Old Money," and meanwhile Margaret released his hand and took a seat and started in talking about pens. The man opened his refrigerator, which was as overloaded as the apartment, another image from the tape now corrupted by squalor. "You poor people, stuck with those awful patches and yet I suppose I wouldn't have the benefit of your company today without them! Ah, well. Here, I wasn't expecting visitors but would you like some cheese? Can I fix you a glass of water?" The man set out a crumbled hunk of cheddar with a butterknife, crumbs on the dish and so long uncovered the edges were dried a deep, translucent orange. "So, you were just Advertising and you thought you'd pay a house call? How am I so lucky?" "Well, that's not it exactly—" Margaret took the knife and began paring away the edges of the cheese, carving out a chunk that looked more or less edible and when she handed it to him he couldn't resist, but tried talking through the mouthful anyway, desperately trying to negotiate the three priorities of hunger, Advertising, and his investigation: "Would you consider, mmmpphh, excuse me, consider opening a nice tall bottle of Very Old Money and settling in to watch this videotape I brought with me because there's something I'd like you to see, a question I've got about it—" The man in the robe nodded absently, half-listening, staring oddly at Margaret and then said, "By all means let me see your tape—is it about beer? I'd be delighted but no hurry, please relax and enjoy yourselves, I'll be right out," and stepped into the living room, began rummaging among his possessions of which there certainly were plenty. It was a little depressing how full the once glorious apartment had gotten. He envisioned himself living in it and cleaning it out, restoring it to the condition on the realtor's tape. Margaret cut him another piece of cheese and whispered, "Do you think he knows something?" "I can't know he seems so nice, well if not nice then harmless, hapless, but I'll judge his reaction to the video, watch him closely when the time comes—" grabbing more cheese quickly while he could and then the man in the robe was back. "Hello, friends, enjoying yourselves?" His robe had fallen open and they both stared but maybe it was just an example of his sloppiness. Certainly there was no polite way to mention it. There was something confusing about this man, who now went to the table and took the knife out of Margaret's hands and held her hand there for a moment and then snapped something, was it a bracelet? around her wrist. Not a bracelet. Handcuffs. "Hey, wait a minute, that's no way to enjoy a nice glass of lager!" he heard himself say idiotically cheese falling out of his mouth jumping up as the man clicked Margaret's other wrist into the cuffs and he had her linked to the back of her chair. He stood to intervene and the man in the robe swept his feet out from under him with a kick and pushed him in the chest and he fell, feet sliding on papers, hand skidding in lumps of cheese, to the floor. "Thirsty!" he shouted, the more excited the more fervent the Advertising, apparently. "No! Beer!" as he struggled to get up. And Margaret was saying something desperate about Eiger Fountain Pens "—*self-refilling cartridge*—" The man in the robe moved quickly, not lazy and sloppy at all now and kicked away his satchel with the tape inside and bent over him and reached behind his ear to tear the patch away, another momentary sting. He could only shout "Beer!" once more before the twilight world of the One-Way Permeable

73

Barrier surrounded him, it was everywhere here, even Margaret was on the other side as long as she wore the patch, and he felt his voice sucked away to a scream audible inside the space of his own head but not elsewhere, he knew, not until he was back outside, on the street where he belonged. And why couldn't he have stayed there? What was he thinking? Anyway it wouldn't be long now because through the gauze he saw the man in the robe who you'd have to call the man half out of his robe now open the door to let the robot in, then as the naked man grinned at him steel pinchers clamped onto his arm and he was dragged out of the room, screaming inaudibly, thrashing to no purpose, leaving Margaret behind. And his tape besides.

Light and the Sufferer

My brother showed me the gun. I'd never seen one up close before. He kept it in a knapsack under his bed at the Y. He held it out and I looked at the black metal.

"You want me to hold it?" I said.

"What, at the place?"

"No, I mean now. I mean, do you want me to touch it or something. Now, I mean like, get comfortable with it."

He stared.

"Don't look at me like I'm crazy. What do you want me to do with the gun?"

"Nothing. I'm just showing it to you, like 'Look, I got it.' Like, 'Here's the gun.'"

My brother was two years younger than me. I was just back from dropping out of my junior year of college, at Santa Cruz, and was living, quite unhappily, at my parents' tiny new house in Plainview, Long Island.

Our parents, Jimmy and Marilla, had kicked Don out for the final time while I was away at school. They hadn't heard from him for almost a year. I went and hung out at Washington Square and found him within a few hours.

"Okay," I said. "Right. Nice gun."

"Don't get freaked."

"I'm not freaked, Don." I paused.

"Then let's go, right?"

"Let's go, Don," I said, and I swear I almost added: *This is good, we're brothers, we still do things together*. I almost said: *See, Don*.

Our parents named my brother Donovan because all their friends had already named their kids Dylan, I guess. It wasn't important to Don. His only chance of ever hearing Donovan was if MC Death sampled "Season of the Witch" or "Hurdy Gurdy Man" in a rap.

Myself being a bit older, I knew those songs in their original versions, not from the radio, of course, but from the days when our parents still played their records.

I followed my brother downstairs. It was night. We walked the short distance to Washington Square Park but stopped half a block away. I stopped.

"What?" said Don.

"Nothing. Should we call the airport? Find out—"

"Like you said, there's always gonna be a plane, Paul."

We went into the park, through the evening throngs, the chessplayers and skatebladers, and I stood on the pathway waiting, shrugging off offers of nickel bags, while Don found his two friends, the ones who were supposed to kill him for stealing drugs.

"—gotta *talk* to you."

"Randall sick of yo shit, Light."

"Can we go up to your apartment, Kaz? Please?"

Don walked them towards me. A fat black man with a gigantic knitted hat: Kaz. Another black man, smaller in every way, with a little beard, and wearing a weirdly glossy, puffed-out gold coat: Drey.

Nobody my brother knew had a regular name. And they all called him "Light," for his being white, I suppose.

"The fuck is this?" said Drey, looking at me.

"Paul," Don mumbled.

76

"Looks like yo fuckin' brother, man."

"All us white dudes look like brothers to you, nigger."

Drey grinned, then tightened his mouth, as though remembering that he was supposed to be angry at Don.

We walked out of the park, east on Third Street. All the way Kaz mumbled at Don: "Can't believe you, man; you fuckin' come around here; you took Randall; can't believe you, man; fuck you think you doin'; look at you stupid face; you think you talk you way out of this; I should be doin' you; fuckin' crackhead; can't believe you man." Et cetera.

And Don just kept saying, every thirty seconds or so: "Shut up, Kaz, man." Or: "Gimme a minute, man."

We went into a door beside a storefront on First Avenue, and up a flight of stairs. Don and I ahead of Kaz and Drey, through the dark.

Kaz stepped around and let us in, and I looked down and saw Don take the gun out of his coat. Don wanted to pull it coming in; he'd said he knew that Kaz kept guns in the house. But not on his person. That was crucial.

We all got inside and Kaz closed the door, and Don turned around. "You're dead," said the fat black man the minute he saw the gun.

The place was just about empty: crumbling walls, a bed. And a cheap safe, nailed instead of bolted to the floor, price tag still showing. A safe house, literally. Crash and stash, as Don would say.

Don waved the gun between Kaz and Drey. "You're dead," said Kaz again. Drey said: "Shit."

"Shut up. Paul, take their shit. Clean Drey up, then Kaz. Find the keys on Kaz."

I stepped up to play my part. Keys on Kaz. I put my hand on Drey, who hissed: "Motherfucker." It turned out the weird shiny gold coat was on inside out; the gold was the *lining* of a rabbit-fur fake leopard. Strange. I ran my hands through the fur, searching out Drey's pockets.

I found a wad, singles on the outside, which I pocketed. Then an Exacto knife, which I tossed on the floor behind me, at Don's feet. He kicked it to the wall.

When I turned to Kaz he slapped my hands away, a strangely girlish move.

"You a chump, Light," he said, ignoring me. "Randall shoulda killed your ass already. He gonna now."

"We're all Randall's chumps, Kaz, man. Now I'm taking and you can tell Randall what you want."

"I ain't no chump, man, Light. You the chump. Randall tried to treat you right. You fuckin' smokehead. You could be playing with the cash like me, like Randall says. 'Staid you *usin'*.'" He hurled the word like it was the only real insult he knew.

It was true. Don had used the drugs he was supposed to deal for Randall.

"Playing with the cash now, Kaz."

I reached for Kaz's pockets again, and again he slapped me away. "You dead, brother."

Don stepped up and clapped Kaz's temple with the side of the gun.

"Ain't no cash, Light, man," Kaz whimpered. He looked down. "Ain't sold it yet, you stupid fuck."

"Open the safe."

"What did you mean 'You dead, *brother*,'?" I asked. "Don told you I'm not his brother. Or are you just using that as an expression?"

Kaz just shook his head and got out the key to the safe. Drey said: "Fuckin' idiot."

Inside the safe was all bottles. Crack. Nothing else. Two big plastic bags full of ten- and five-dollar bottles. I'd never seen that much in one place. Don had, of course; specifically, when Kaz and Randall brought him up here to entrust him with a load of bottles to sell.

That time there had also been a large supply of cash, which was what we were here supposedly to steal.

"Fuck you expected?" said Drey.

"You dead," said Kaz.

Don didn't hesitate. He took the two bags of bottles and quickly felt behind them, but there was nothing else in the safe. He slammed the door shut and pushed the gun up at Kaz's face again. "Your roll, Kaz."

"You a fuckin' chump." Kaz got out his money, another fat wad with ones on the outside. Don took it and stuffed it in his pocket. Then he shook the two bags of bottles into the two big side pockets of his parka, tossing the plastic bags aside when they were empty.

"Fuck you gonna do?" said Drey. "Sell the shit? Randall gun you down."

"Gimme the keys," said Don to Kaz. "Sit down. Both of you."

"Shit."

Don waved the gun some more, and Kaz and Drey sat down on the floor. Don pushed me back out into the hallway ahead of him, then shut the door and locked it from the outside with Kaz's key.

That was when we saw the Sufferer. It was sitting on the landing of the stairway above us, looking down. On its haunches in the dark it looked just like a giant panther, eyes shining.

I assumed it was waiting for someone else. I'd only seen the aliens twice before, each time trailing after somebody in trouble. That was what they liked to do.

Don didn't even glance at it. I guess leading his lifestyle, he passed them pretty often. He put the gun in his belt and ran downstairs, and I followed him. The Sufferer padded down after us.

Don hailed a cab on First Avenue. "La Guardia," he said, leaning in the window.

"Manhattan only," said the cabbie. Don pulled out Kaz's money and began peeling off ones. I looked behind us, thinking of Kaz and Drey and the unlocated guns in the apartment. Had Don really locked them in? Even if he had, they could shoot us from the front windows, or off the fire escape, while we haggled with the cabbie.

I saw the Sufferer push out of the door and settle on the sidewalk to watch us.

"Fifteen dollars before the fare," said Don. "C'mon."

The driver popped the locks, and Don and I scooted into the back, Don's coat-load of bottles clinking against the door.

"La Guardia," said Don again.

"Take the Manhattan Bridge," I said. "Canal Street."

"He knows where the Manhattan Bridge is, Paul."

"He said Manhattan only."

"You picking somebody up?" said the driver.

"Domestic departures," I said.

"What airline?"

"Uh, Pan Am."

"There is no more Pan Am," said the driver.

"Wow. Okay, uh, Delta?"

"Does it matter?" said Don.

"He has to take us *somewhere*," I explained patiently. Sometimes it seemed like Don and I grew up in separate universes. "The airport is big. Delta should have a lot of flights to California. We can start there, anyway."

The cab went down First to Canal and entered the funnel

of traffic leading onto the bridge. I always mention the Manhattan Bridge because a lot of people just reflexively take the Brooklyn, though it isn't really faster or more convenient. People prefer the Brooklyn Bridge, I guess because it's prettier, but I like the way you can be driving alongside a *subway train* on the Manhattan Bridge.

So I looked out the window, and what I saw was the Sufferer, running alongside the cab, keeping time even when the traffic smoothed out and we accelerated across the empty middle of the bridge. It loped along right beside us, almost under my window. Our cabbie was going faster than the other cars, and when we passed one the Sufferer would drop back, trailing us, until the space beside my door was clear again.

Don was in his own world, leafing through the roll he'd stolen and counting the bottles in his pockets by feel. I didn't draw his attention to the Sufferer. The cabbie hadn't noticed either.

"You can't take the gun on the plane," I said to Don, quietly.

"Big news," said Don sarcastically.

"It's okay," I said, responding to his annoyance as some kind of plea for reassurance, as I always had. "We won't need it in Cali."

"Yeah," he said dreamily.

"We're really going," I said. "Things'll be different there." I felt it slipping away, the hold my proposal had had on him an hour ago.

"What," he snorted. "Nobody has guns in California?"

"You're going to live different, there." I looked up to see if the cabbie was listening. "So why don't you leave the gun here in the cab, okay, Don? Just push it under the seat. Because it's crazy going into the airport with it. Crazy enough just carrying all the drugs."

"I'll put it in a locker. Just in case."

"What? In case of what?"

We pulled off onto the BQE and headed for the airport. I checked the window. There was the Sufferer, rushing along with us, leaping potholes.

"What?" said Don, noticing.

"One of those aliens."

"The one from Kaz's?"

I shrugged—a lie, since I knew. "How much money did you get from Kaz?" I said, trying to change the subject.

"Four hundred. Chump change from a chump. Fuck is it doing out there?" He leaned over me to look out the window.

"Hey," said the cabbie. "You got a Sufferer."

"Just drive," said Don.

"I don't want trouble. Why's it following you?"

"It's not following anyone," I said. "Anyway, they don't cause trouble. They *prevent* it. They keep people out of trouble."

"Right. So if they follow you, you must be trouble."

Don took the gun out of his belt, but kept it below the level of the Plexiglas barrier above the seat. I tried to scowl at him, but he ignored me.

"You don't like it, why don't you try to kill it with the car?" he said to the driver in a low, insinuating voice.

"You're crazy."

"Right. So just take us to the airport and shut up." He looked at me. "How much you get?"

"Two hundred and fifty dollars. Sidekick change from a sidekick." The joke was out before I thought to wonder: but who's the sidekick *here*? It was possibly a very important question.

Don snorted. "Barely afford the tickets." He put the gun back into his belt.

The Sufferer accompanied us through the maze of exits and into the roundabout of the airport. We pulled up in front of Delta. Don paid the cabfare and rolled off twenty extra, then paused, and rolled off another twenty. "Pull up there and wait ten minutes," he said.

"Don, we're getting on a plane. Besides, even if we weren't, it isn't hard to catch a cab at the *airport*."

"Just in case. Me and this dude got an understanding. Right, man?" He cocked his head at the driver.

The cabbie shrugged, then smiled. "Sure. I'll wait."

I sighed. Don was always turning passerby into accomplices. Even when it didn't mean anything. It was a kind of compulsive seduction, like *Women Who Love Too Much*.

"You're getting me worried, Don. We're flying out of here, right?"

"Relax. We're at the airport, right? Just wait a minute." He put his mouth at the driver's little money window. "Pull up over there, man. We'll walk back, we don't have bags or anything. Just get out of the light, okay?"

We pulled past the terminal entrance, into a dead zone of baggage carts. The Sufferer trotted alongside, on the pedestrian ramp, weaving around the businessmen and tourists leaking out of the terminal.

Don rolled his window down a couple of inches, then got out a glass pipe and shook out the contents of a five-dollar vial into the bowl.

"Donnie."

"Hey, not in the cab!"

"Minute, man." He flicked his lighter and the little rocks flared blue and pink and disappeared. So practiced, so fast.

The Sufferer leaned close in to my window and watched.

When Don noticed he said: "Open your door and whack that fuckin' thing in the face."

"Don't smoke that crap in my cab," said the driver.

"Okay, okay," said Don, palming the pipe away. He pointed a finger at the cabbie. "You'll wait, right?"

"I'll wait, but don't do that in my cab."

"Let's go, Don."

"Okay."

I opened my door and the Sufferer stepped aside to let us pass. We got out onto the walkway. Don stopped and shook his head, straightened his parka, which was burdened with the loaded pockets, and pushed the gun out of sight under his sweatshirt. We walked up to the entrance. The doors were operated by electric eye, and they slid open for us, then stayed open as the Sufferer followed.

Don and I both instinctively hurried into a mass of people, but no crowd could have been big enough to keep it from being obvious who the alien was with. A baggage guy stood and watched, his eyes going from the Sufferer to us and back again. He could as easily have been airport security—maybe he was.

"We've got a problem here, Don," I said.

"Yeah." He made a mugging face, but didn't meet my eye.

"Let's—here, you've gotta find a place for the gun, anyway." I steered him out of the flow near the ticket agents, to a relatively empty stretch of terminal: newspaper vending machines, hotel phones, and a shoeshine booth. I didn't see any lockers, though.

The Sufferer sat and cocked its head at us, waiting.

"What do your friends do when this happens?"

"What?" said Don sarcastically. "You mean when some big black animal from space follows them to the airport after an armed robbery?"

84

"When these things—when one of these things shows up, Don. I mean, it must happen to people you know."

"One dude, Rolando. Thing started trailing him. Rolando fell in love, like him and the thing fucking eloped. Last I saw Rolando. Just that one dude, though."

As people passed us they'd stare first at the Sufferer, then follow its gaze to us.

"Ironic," I said. "It wants to help you, right? At least, I assume so. But it doesn't know that you're planning to go to California to dry out. It probably doesn't even understand how airports work, how it's fucking this up for you. How important it is for you to leave the city."

I was babbling. I couldn't help myself. I wanted to hear him say *Yes, I mean to get on a plane and change my life in California, Paul. You had a good idea*. Instead of his grunting, distracted assent. It didn't help that his big last farewell heist had netted pockets full of crack instead of cash.

And I didn't for the life of me know what to do with the Sufferer.

"It doesn't want to help me," Don said.

"Yeah, well, in this case, anyway, it isn't. We're already gonna fit a bad profile, buying tickets at the last minute with cash. If there's a Sufferer trailing around they'll search us for sure."

"They let it on the plane?"

"I don't think so. I mean, how could they? So all we have to do is dump the drugs *and* the gun, then they can search us all they want, doesn't matter, we're gone."

"Uh-uh."

"What?"

"I'm on parole, Paul. Breaking parole to go. I can't get checked out."

"What? You never told me you were in prison!"

"Shut up, Paul. *Sentenced* to parole, one year. Nothing, man."

"For what?"

"*Nothing,* man. Now shut up. What, you think I wasn't breaking the *law?*"

"Okay, okay, but listen, we just have to get on a plane. We have to try. So stash the stuff—"

"Nah. This is no good. I got an idea." He headed back to the terminal exits.

"Don!"

The Sufferer and I followed him out. He jogged back to the cab, hands protectively over the flaps of his coat pockets. We got back in and Don said: "Get us out of here."

"Back."

"Yeah, that direction. But get off the fuckin' freeway."

"Have to be on the freeway—"

"Yeah, yeah, I mean as soon as you can."

I actually thought we'd lost the Sufferer when we exited into a blasted neighborhood of boarded-up and gutted storefronts, but by the time we'd driven, at Don's request, back under the freeway and into a dark, empty cobblestone lot, the alien came loping up behind us.

The freeway roared above us, but the nearby streets were vacant. The people in the cars might as well have been in flying saucers, whistling past stragglers in the desert.

Don gave the cabbie another ten and said: "Get lost for fifteen minutes. Leave us here and circle around, find yourself a cup of coffee or something." The cabbie and I exchanged a look that said *Coffee? Here?* but Don was already out of the cab.

I got out and the cab rumbled away over the cobblestones and around a corner. The Sufferer didn't glance at it, just sat like an obedient dog and watched us.

Don ignored it, or pretended to, and walked over and took a seat on the fender of a wrecked truck. It was getting cold. I thought, stupidly, about the meal we would have been eating, about the movie we would have been watching, on the plane.

Don took out the pipe again and loaded it with a rock of crack. The wind bent the blue column of flame from his lighter one way, then Don sucked it the other, into the pipe. The Sufferer hurried up like a hunting cat to where Don sat. I stepped back.

Don curled his shoulder protectively around the pipe and glared back at the alien. "Fuck *you* want?"

The Sufferer nudged at his elbow with its hand-like paw.

"Leave me the fuck alone."

"Don, what are you doing? It can't help it. What are you trying to do, bait it?"

Don ignored me. He flicked his lighter again, tried to get a hit. The Sufferer jogged his elbow. Don kicked at it. The alien danced back easily out of the way, like a boxer, then stepped back in, trying to square its face with Don's, trying to look him in the eye.

Don kicked out again, brushing the Sufferer back, then pocketed the pipe and drew out his gun.

The alien cocked his head.

"Hey, Don—"

Don fired the gun straight into the Sufferer's chest, and the alien jumped back and fell onto the cobblestones, then got back on its feet and walked in a little circle, shaking its head, blinking its eyes.

Don said: "Ow, fuck, I think I sprained my arm."

"How? What happened?"

"The gun, man. It bucked back on me. Shit."

"You can't kill it, Don. Everybody knows that. The shots'll just bring the police."

Don looked at me. His expression was dazed and cynical at the same time. "I just wanted to give it a piece of my fuckin' mind, okay, Paul?"

"Okay, Don. Now what about going back to the airport?"

"Nah. We gotta lose this thing."

The Sufferer circled back around to where Don sat still holding the gun, kneading his injured forearm with his free hand. The alien sat up like a perky cat and tapped at Don's jacket pocket, rattling the load of bottles.

"I guess it just wants to see you get clean, Don. If you get rid of the bottles it'll leave us alone and we can fly to California."

"You believe that shit, Paul? Where'd you read that, *Newsweek?*"

"What?"

"That this thing is like some kind of vice cop? That it wants me to kick?"

"Isn't that the idea?" The stuff I'd read about them wasn't clear on much except that they followed users around, actually.

"Yeah? Watch this." Don clicked the safety on the gun and handed it to me, then got out his pipe and loaded it. He braised the rock with flame from the lighter, but this time when he got it glowing he turned it around and offered it to the Sufferer. The alien grasped the pipe in its dexterous paw and stuck the end in its mouth and toked.

"I think I read about that," I said, lying. "It's like an empathy thing. They want to earn your trust."

Don just smirked at me, then snatched his pipe away from the Sufferer, who didn't protest.

"I'm cold," I said. "You think that cab is coming back?"

"Fuck yes," said Don. "You kidding? We're a fucking gold mine." He shook out another rock.

The Sufferer and I both watched. Suddenly I wanted some. I'd done a lot of uncooked coke with some of my Upper West Side friends the last year of high school, but I'd only smoked rock twice before, with Don each time.

"Give me a hit, Don," I said.

He loaded the pipe and handed it and the lighter to me, ungrudgingly.

I drew in a hit, and felt the crazy rush of the crack hit me. Like snorting a line of coke while plummeting over the summit of a roller coaster.

The Sufferer opened its weird, toothless black mouth and leaned towards me, obviously wanting another hit.

"Maybe the idea is to help run through your stash," I said. "Help use up your stuff, keep you from O.D.ing. Because their bodies can take it, like the bullets. Doesn't hurt them."

"Maybe they're just fucking crackheads, Paul."

The cab's reappearance startled me, the sound of its approach masked by the rush of cars overhead. And of course, I was thinking of cops.

Don took his gun back, jammed it in his waistband, and we got into the back. Don held the door open for the Sufferer. "Might as well get it off the freeway," he said. "Gonna be with us next place we go either way." The Sufferer didn't hesitate to clamber in over our feet and settle down on the floor of the back, pretty much filling the space.

"Okay, but we need a plan, Donnie." I heard myself beginning to whine.

"Where to?" said the cabbie.

"Back to Manhattan," said Don. "East, uh, 83rd and, uh, Park." He turned to me. "Chick I know."

"You can't go back to the city."

"Manhattan is a big place, Paul. Far as Randall and Kaz is concerned, 83rd Street might as well be California."

"Don't talk to me about California. Like you know something about California."

"Paul, man, I didn't say shit about California. I'm just saying we can hide out uptown, figure some shit out, okay? Take care of the Crackhead from Space here, right?"

"Uptown. New York is a world to you, you don't know anything but uptown or downtown or Brooklyn. California's a whole other place, Donnie, you can't imagine. It'll be *different*. The things you're dealing with here, they don't have to be—you don't have to have these *issues*, Donnie. Randall, uptown, whatever."

"Okay, Paul. But I just wanna take care of two things, okay, and then we'll go, let's just get rid of the Creature and just move this stuff to some people I know, okay? Get cash for this product, then we'll go."

The Sufferer shifted, stepping on my foot, and looked up at us.

"Okay." I was defeated, by the two of them. It was like they were in collusion now. "Just don't talk about California like it's *Mars*, for God's sake. We're going there, you'll see how it is, and then you can tell me what you think. It'll blow your mind, Donnie, to see how different it can be."

"Yeah," he said, far away.

We were silent into Manhattan. At 83rd Street and Park Avenue Don paid the cab fare, and we got out. The three of us. The street was full of cars, mainly cabs, actually—nobody up here owned a car—but the side-walk was dead, except for doormen. In a way Don was right about New York. This was another place. The thought of him selling crack on Park Avenue gave me a quick laugh.

Don led us into a brightly lit foyer. "Annette Sweeney," he told the doorman.

The doorman eyed the Sufferer. "Is she expecting visitors?"

"Tell her it's Light."

We went up to the ninth floor and found Annette Sweeney's door. Annette Sweeney lived well—I knew that before we even got inside.

She opened the door before we could knock. "You can't just always come up here, Light."

"Annette, chill out. I got some stuff for you. If it's not a good time—"

Annette baited easily. Don's hook gave me an idea what they had in common. "No, Light, I'm just saying why don't you call? Why don't you *ever* call me? What do you have?"

"Just some stuff." He stepped in. "This my brother."

"Hi." She was staring at the Sufferer. "Light, look."

"I know. Forget it."

I stepped in, and so did the Sufferer. Like it owned the place.

"What do you mean? When did this happen?"

"Shut up, forget it. It's a temporary thing."

"What did you do?"

Don went past her, left the rest of us in the doorway, and flopped on her couch. The apartment was big and spare, the architectural detail as lush as the outside of the building, the furniture modern, all aluminum and glass.

"I haven't seen you for weeks, Annette. What did I do? I did a lot of shit, you want to know it all? I come here and you ask me questions?"

Annette fazed easily. She tilted her head so that her hair fell, then brushed it away and pursed her lips and said: "*Sorry*, Light." I saw a rich girl who thought that when she hung out with my brother she was slumming. And I saw my brother twisting her incredible need around his fingers, and hated them both for a second.

Then she turned to me and smiled weakly and said: "Hi. I'm Annette . . . I didn't know Light had a brother," and I felt immediately guilty for judging. It didn't hurt that she was beautiful, really striking, with black hair and big black eyes.

I took her hand. The Sufferer pushed past us, brushing my hip, and leapt onto the couch beside Don. "Yeah, well, he does," I said. "I'm Paul."

"It's funny, 'cause my brother is staying with me right now. That's why I was so weird about Light just dropping by."

"You got a brother?" said Don, distractedly. He'd pulled all the little bottles out of his pockets and piled them on her rug. The Sufferer just sat upright on the couch and watched him.

"Yeah. He's out right now, but he might come back."

"That's cool," said Don. "We'll party."

"Um, Douglas might not really wanna . . . *Jesus*, Light."

"What?"

"Well, just—your new friend. And all that stuff."

"I guess the two kind of go together," I said.

"Very funny," said Don. "He's harmless, he's our—what, *mascot*. Like Tony the Tiger. Smoke rock—it's grrrreat!"

"Doesn't it freak you out?"

"Nah." Don chucked the Sufferer on the chin. "You can't believe all that shit you hear. It just wants to hang. That's all they want. Came from space to party with me. You should of seen it following the cab, though—it was like a video game."

Annette shook her head, grinning.

"Hey, Paul, come here for a minute," said Don, jumping up, nodding his head at the door to the bedroom.

"What?"

"Nothing. Lemme talk to you for a minute though."

We left Annette and the drugs and the Sufferer in the living room, and sat on the edge of the bed. "Don't talk about this California thing," Don said in a low voice. "Don't let Annette hear about us leaving because she'll fucking flip out if she hears I'm going away and I don't need that, okay?"

"Okay," I said, then: "Don?"

"What?"

"Maybe we should call Jimmy and Marilla. Let them know you're okay."

"They kicked me out. They don't care."

"Just because they couldn't let you live there anymore doesn't mean they don't worry about you. Just to let them know you're still *alive*—"

"Okay, but later, okay?" He had a distracted expression, one I was beginning to recognize: *I want a hit*.

"Okay."

Don tapped me on the back and we went back out. The Sufferer had the pipe, but Annette looked like she'd had possession of it recently enough. The room was filled with that sour ozone smell.

She didn't ask what we'd been talking about in private. Didn't even seem to wonder. In general, her self-esteem around my brother seemed kind of low.

"Here," said Don, plucking the pipe away from the alien. I knelt down on the carpet with them and accepted the offer. Between Don and Annette and the Sufferer it was seriously questionable whether any of the drugs would get sold— which was fine with me. Whether or not using up Don's supply was part of the alien's strategy—assuming the alien had a strategy—didn't matter. It could be my strategy.

Annette got up and found her cigarettes and brought one back lit, adding to the haze. Then she brushed her hair back and, seemingly emboldened by the cocaine and nicotine, began talking. "Really, though, Light, you should look out, with this thing hanging around you. I heard about how there are people who'll beat you up just because you've got one of these things following you around. It's a reactionary thing, like AIDS-bashing, you know, blaming the victim. Also won't the police, like, search you or something, hassle you, if they see it?"

"The police know me. They already hassle me. I don't mean shit to the police. Tony the Tiger doesn't change that."

"It's just weird, Light."

"Of course it's weird," said Don. "That's why we love it, right, Paul? It's from another dimension, it's fucking weird, it's science fiction." The Sufferer cocked its head at Don as if it was considering his words. Don raised his fists like a boxer. The Sufferer opened its mouth at him, a black O, and its ears, or what I was mistaking for its ears, wrinkled forward. Now that I could see it up close, it really didn't look so much like a cat. The face was really more human, like the sphinx with a toothless octopus mouth.

Don waved his hands in its face and said: "Dee-nee dee-nee, dee-nee dee-nee"—Twilight Zone Theme.

"Well, when's it going to leave you alone?" She took another rock of crack and stuffed it into the end of an unlit cigarette.

"I'm gonna lose it," he said.

"That's supposed to be pretty hard, Light. I mean, it's like an *obsession* for them."

"Would you stop quoting the, whatever, the Geraldo Rivera version, or wherever you got that crap? I said I'm gonna lose it. You can help. We can trap it in your bedroom and I'll cut out."

"I think it can hear you, Don," I said.

"That's so fucking stupid, man. It's from another planet."

Of course we all turned to look at it now. It stared back and then pawed at the pile of bottles on the carpet.

"Hey, cut it out," said Don. He reached out to push it away, then winced. "Fuck."

"What?"

"You think you could rub my arm? I sprained it or something." He reached under his sweatshirt and freed himself of the gun, dropping it with a clatter on a little table beside the couch.

"Uh, sure, Light," Annette said absently, goggling at the gun. She put her cigarette in her mouth and scooted up beside Don and took his arm in her lap. The Sufferer went on rattling the bottles.

"What about at the airport?" Don said. "You didn't think it could understand us then."

"I'm wrong, it was just a feeling."

"Why'd you have to say that? You creeped me the fuck out."

"Airport?" said Annette.

"Uh, that's where we had to go to get the stuff," I said, gesturing at the rug, taking up the burden of covering Don's slip out of guilt, out of habit.

"You scored at the *airport?*"

Don shrugged at her, and said: "Sure."

Annette lit the loaded cigarette. The rock hissed as it hit the flame. "What are you doing with all this?"

"Well, I really gotta sell some," said Don. "I was wondering if you wanted to call some of your friends. I don't wanna go downtown now."

"I don't know, Light." She looked at the Sufferer, who was still rattling at the vials. "Won't it narc on us?"

"Don't be stupid."

"Even if it doesn't, that's what everybody'll think if they see it here."

"Just set it up, okay? We can arrange something so they don't have to meet Tony the Tiger." He lit a rock and toked.

"Well, anyway, my brother is coming back tonight so I don't think you can deal out of my house, Light."

"What does that have to do with it? It's *your* house, right?"

"Well, I don't know. He's my *older* brother."

"Paul is my older fucking brother," Don said. "So what?"

Maybe Annette's older brother knows how to take care of his sibling, I thought. Like I obviously don't.

There was a sound of a key fumbling in a lock. "Speak of the devil," said Annette.

Douglas turned out to be quite a bit older than Annette, or at least the way he dressed and held himself made it seem that way. He came up to where we all were sprawled on the couch and the carpet and said, to me: "Are you Light?"

"No," said Don, "that's me."

Douglas's eyes played over the scene: the gun, the vials, the alien sitting like a giant snake-skinned cougar on the carpet.

He reached down and picked up the gun.

"Ann, why don't you go lock yourself in the bedroom," he said.

"*Doug*-las," she whined.

"Do it."

"Don't be a chump," said Don. "This is her place."

"Shut up. I know all about you. We're going to have a little talk. *Go*, Ann."

96

"I told you," Annette said to Don as she got up from the couch. "Uh, nice to meet you, Paul. Sorry."

As she slouched her way to the bedroom, the Sufferer jumped up and followed her. Douglas took a step back, startled. I watched the gun. Douglas handled it badly, but I was pretty sure the safety was still in place.

The Sufferer was suddenly, inexplicably agitated. It ran ahead of her into the bedroom, looked out the far window at the lights of the building across 83rd Street, and back at us.

"What's it doing?" said Doug angrily.

Don shrugged. Annette stood waiting at the doorway.

"Get it out of there," said Doug, gesturing with the gun.

"Hey, that's not my responsibility," said Don. "You're the dude who's taking charge."

The Sufferer wrinkled its ears forward and stared glumly at Don. Don glowered at Douglas.

"Here," I said. I went in and pushed at the Sufferer. Its flesh was like a dense black pudding, and it felt like it weighed about a thousand pounds. I tried to prod it towards the door, but it wouldn't budge. Annette came into the bedroom and tried to help me push, to no avail.

Don, his movements exaggerated and slow, put a rock of coke into the glass pipe and flicked his lighter enticingly. The Sufferer trotted forward, like it had read the script, and Annette and I almost fell on our faces.

Douglas didn't find it funny. "Get back out here," he said to me, and when I obliged he reached over and slammed the door shut with Annette inside. "Sit down," he told me, and I did it.

The Sufferer, of course, paid him no mind. It went past us all, into the kitchen.

"What's on your mind?" said Don drawlingly, lighting the pipe.

"I want you and your monster out of Annette's life, *Light*," said Douglas. "She's told me plenty about you."

"Why not? I'm her boyfriend."

"You're not her boyfriend," snarled Douglas. "You're her dealer. Only you're not even around enough to do a good job of that." From the kitchen came a crash of breaking glass. Douglas looked in, then turned back to Don. "You get Annette hooked and then she's gotta go out and find her own because you smoked up your whole shipment. You pathetic piece of human garbage."

"Fuck told you that shit?"

"What, is it a shock to find out that you're known, you sleazeball?"

Another crash from the kitchen, and then a sound like chimes: the Sufferer wading through the glass or ceramic it had broken.

"What's your—monster-thing doing?" said Douglas. I got the feeling that his castigating Don was the fulfillment of a long-standing fantasy, only the Sufferer wasn't part of the scenario.

"I told you, it's not my thing, I don't tell it what to do, man."

"Is that why you're trying to unload all this stuff on my sister—the monster won't let you use it anymore?"

Don just smirked. "The monster's 'using it' with me. I don't tell it what to do and it don't tell me what to do."

"It's following you because you're dead, you loser. You're smoking your life away—it's like your death angel."

"That's not right," I said. "It's nothing like that. It's an empathy thing, it's responding to the *life* in Don—"

"Yeah, right. The life. You people are walking corpses. And I'll finish you off myself if you don't leave my sister alone."

"You wanna kill me, huh?" said Don.

"I will if I have to. Before you destroy my sister's life like you destroyed your own. Before one of those death creatures comes prowling around for her."

"You don't know what you're talking about," I said.

"You never met a Sufferer before, you have no idea how they operate."

"You never met me before, either," said Don.

"I heard all I need to know from your sleazebag pusher friends," said Douglas.

"What?" said Don, suddenly attentive.

"When you disappeared, Annette started buying from this black dude who called around for you. Real pimpy type of guy. I had to call the cops on him. I *should* call the cops on you."

"Who—Annette!" Don jumped up.

"Randall," said Douglas. "Randall whose shipment you singlehandedly smoked up. I'm surprised you're not dead by now."

Annette looked out of the bedroom. "You gave him my number, Light, remember? He called here looking for you about, I don't know, four or five days ago—"

"Let's get the fuck out of here," said Don. "Give me my gun." He knelt down and began scooping the vials back into his parka.

"Take your crap with you," said Douglas. "Go get nice and high on it. But I think I'd better keep the gun."

"*Fuck* you, man—"

"No, fuck *you*." Douglas clicked the safety off. I was surprised he knew how. Then he put his foot on Don's shoulder and shoved him back on his ass on the carpet. "No more bullshit, Light. You leave Annette alone, no calls, no late-night visits, got it? And I'm keeping the gun. You're lucky I don't call the cops."

"Call the cops, see if I give a damn, man. You don't have a fucking clue." Don stood up. He came up to Douglas's shoulder, but he was crowding the gun, and Douglas took a step back. I thought about trying to step in and realized my whole body was trembling.

The Sufferer came out of the kitchen, pumping forward on its massive black legs, and rushed up to where Douglas stood. It opened its strange black mouth and emitted a sound, something between a howl and a moan. Actually, it sounded like a man bellowing as he fell down a bottomless well, complete with echoes and Doppler effects.

At the same time chunks of broken glass fell out of its mouth at Douglas's feet, and on his shoes.

Douglas pointed the gun and fired, at almost the exact same spot on the alien's big bulldog chest. The noise, in the quiet apartment, was deafening. Douglas dropped the weapon and grabbed his hand, wincing.

Don immediately picked it up.

"Go," he said to me, and nodded at the door. Then he bent back down to collect the last of his vials, sweeping up the empties along with them.

Douglas stood holding his hand, watching the Sufferer. The creature had rolled back on its haunches at the impact of the gunshot, and now it was shaking its head vigorously, and spitting out more shards of glass.

Don pushed the gun back into his belt and hustled me towards the door, and then turned and slapped Douglas ever so lightly on the cheek. Like he wanted to wake him up, not hurt him. "You mess up your hand?" he said.

Douglas didn't say anything.

"Maybe your sister can rub it for you. See ya."

We ran to the elevator, the Sufferer leaping after us.

Out on the street Don said: "Hell was it doing?"

"It got you your gun back," I said.

"Yeah, but what was it doing, eating the dishes?" He knelt down and looked in the Sufferer's mouth. "Jesus." He reached in and pulled out a chunk of glass that was lodged there. The Sufferer snorted and shook its head.

"It's like the one soft spot, the whatchacallit, Achilles tendon," Don said. "I wonder if I could kill it by shooting it in the mouth?"

"*Donnie!* That's not cool. It saved you up there. Besides, you can't kill them, I read it—"

"Okay, shut up." He tossed the glass out into the street, under a parked car.

"Now what?" I said, and then quickly made my nomination: "The airport? Or Port Authority, catch a Greyhound upstate?"

Don didn't say anything.

"Upstate, New York State, isn't breaking parole, right? You can do anything you want, doesn't matter if the Sufferer's following you. I bet they've never seen one of these guys up there, huh?"

"I gotta sell the shit," said Don. "The triangle on 72nd and Broadway. I can move it there. C'mon, we can walk across." He started towards Central Park.

We ran after him, me and the Sufferer. "Don, wait. Why can't we just go? What are you stalling for?"

"Damn, Paul, you can't just show up with this idea and *rush* me out of town. Maybe I don't *want* to go to California. Maybe at least you ought to let me clear up my damn business before we go, okay?"

"What? *What?*" As if the robbery hadn't happened, or as if it weren't connected to the plan, a plan he'd already agreed to.

"Relax, okay. Damn. We'll go. Just let me unload the stuff, okay?"

We walked to the edge of the park on the empty streets, the three of us. In silence, until Don said, without turning: "It's been a while since we were in touch."

"What? Yeah, I guess. What do you mean?"

"That's all, just it's been a while. We didn't, like, keep up on each other's lives or anything."

"Yeah," I said, chilled.

Central Park at night made me think of high school, of smoking pot with my Upper West Side friends. White people's drugs, drugs for the kids who stay in school, go to college. While back in Brooklyn, Don was finding the other kind, the drugs for the black kids, the ones who wouldn't go to college even if they bluffed it through high school.

Now my West Side friends were all off at college, in various parts of the country, and I was back in town to sell drugs at 72nd and Broadway, under their parents' windows.

The Sufferer seemed to like the park. Several times it roamed wide of us, disappearing briefly in the trees. When we crossed Central Park West, though, it was back close at our heels.

We set up at the benches on the triangle, along with some sleeping winos. There was a black kid, too, who kept crossing the street to the subway and ducking inside, then crossing back to the triangle. He and the Sufferer exchanged a long look, then the kid went back to his pacing routine, and the Sufferer jumped over the bench, into the little plot of land the pavement and benches encircled. I hoped it would stay there, more or less out of sight from the street.

"This is dead, Don."

"Relax. It's where you come, up here. It's the only place to score."

"It's Tuesday night."

"Junkies don't know weekends, man."

"We're gonna get arrested. This is just like a target, like sitting in the middle of a target."

"Shut up. You're being a chump. Forget the cops."

A chump. The unkindest cut. I shut up. Don got out his pipe and smoked away another rock of the product. I had a hit too. The Sufferer didn't seem as interested.

And we waited.

The traffic on Broadway was all cabs, and—surprise!—two of them pulled over and transacted business with Don. One was slumming West Side yuppies on their way to a club, men overdressed, women waiting in the back of the cab, relieved laughter when the males returned safely. The other was two blacks in the front seat, the cabbie and a pal, with the cab still available. I ached to push Don in the back and take off, but I stayed shut up.

Another customer walked up, from the park side. He caught up with the kid, who shook his head, nodded at us, and made his jog across the street to the subway station again while the street was clear. Don made the sale and the guy headed back the way he'd come.

I was just noticing that this time the kid hadn't come back to the triangle when the truck pulled up. A van, really, like a UPS delivery truck but covered with layers of graffiti and minor dents, and missing doors on both sides. It pulled around the triangle the wrong way, bringing down a plague of honking from cabs.

Don said: "Oh shit."

"What?"

"That's Randall's truck." But he didn't move, or reach for the gun.

The driver kicked the emergency brake down and turned

to us holding a toy-like machine gun. I figured it wasn't a toy. "Is that Randall?" I said.

"Nah. Shut up now."

The man in the passenger seat came around the front. Well dressed, unarmed. "Light," he said.

"Yo, Randall."

"Get in the back. This your man?" He raised his chin at me. His voice had a slight Caribbean lilt.

Don shrugged.

"You took my safe house tonight, my man?" Randall asked me. He was clean and pretty, like some young, unbeaten boxer. But he had a boiled-looking finger-thick scar running all along the right underside of his jaw, and where it would have crossed his ear the lobe was missing.

"That's me," I said, dorkily.

"Come along." He made it sound jolly. He opened the back. Inside were Kaz and Drey, sitting on tires, looking miserable.

I tried to catch Don's eye, but he just trudged forward and stepped up into the back. I went after him.

I glanced over my shoulder, but didn't spot the Sufferer. Randall climbed in behind us, slammed the two doors shut, and went up to the front. There wasn't any divider, just a big open metal box with two bucket seats in front of the window, and a steering wheel on a post to the floor. The driver handed Randall the little machine gun and took off across Broadway, down 72nd Street.

Don and I leaned against the back. I looked out the back window and just caught sight of the pay phone on the far side of the subway entrance.

We rattled to the end of 72nd, under the West Side Highway and parked out on the stretch of nothing before the water. It's always amazing to get to the edge of Manhattan and see how much stuff there is between the city—you know, the city that you think of, the city people use—and the real edge of the island. You think of it as being like a raft of skyscrapers, buildings to the edge, and instead there's the edge of the island. Boathouses, concrete and weeds, places that nobody cares about.

Unfortunately, at the moment.

The driver serving as gunman again, Randall opened the back and steered us out into a dark, empty garage, a sort of cinderblock shell full of rusted iron drums and piles of rotting linoleum tile. The floor was littered with glass and twisted, rusty cable. A seagull squawked out of our path, flapping but not taking off, then refolded its wings and wobbled outside once we were safely past. Kaz and Drey both looked back dubiously, acting more like fellow captives than Randall's henchmen, but Randall kept nodding us forward, until the moonlight from the garage entrance petered out and we all stood in darkness.

"You messin' up, Light," said Randall.

"Here's your stuff," said Don, scooping in his parka pockets. He sounded afraid. I wondered where the Sufferer was.

"That's good. Give it to Drey. You make a little green out there?"

"Yeah."

"You smoke up a little, there, too?"

Before Don could squeak "Yeah" again Randall stepped forward and smacked him, viciously hard, across the mouth. Don's foot slipped and skidded through the broken glass, but he kept from falling.

"Relax, relax," said Randall suddenly, as though some protest had been raised. "We ain't killing you tonight, Light. But we gotta talk about this funny stuff, you chumps playing with my money. You think you takin' Kaz but it's all my money, right?"

"Yeah."

"It's like it's all a game, like *Monopoly* money, you and Kaz can just fuckin' *play* with it."

"Kaz didn't do anything wrong," said Don.

"Kaz a sucker get taken by a chump like you." He raised his hand and Kaz flinched. Leaving his hand in the air, he turned to me. "Who's your man here?"

"Paul."

"He your brother?"

"Nah."

Randall looked at Kaz and Drey. "This the dude?"

Kaz nodded.

Randall stared at me, but he was still talking to Don. "You tell him Randall got some easy money, some play money, just laying around? You tell him I'm a fuckin' chump?"

"Randall, we didn't even take your money. Just some dope, man. We only took money off Kaz and Drey."

"My dope *is* money, stupid. My dope is *product*. Not for you to fuckin' smoke. Why you so stupid, crackhead?"

At that moment a shadow slipped in through the moonlit garage entrance, then almost disappeared into the darkness. The Sufferer. I felt relieved, like it was the cavalry. But when it came into the circle it stepped up beside Randall, and then I saw that it wasn't the same. It was bigger than ours, its eyes were longer, slits instead of ovals, and the strangely human nose was pushed to one side. A scarred Sufferer, for Randall.

"Here's my thing," said Randall. "I heard you got a thing, yourself. You been seen around *town* together."

"Uh, yeah. So what?"

"So what? That the only reason I came up here to talk to you myself, you think I bother with a fuckin' chump like you? Only reason my man didn't do you in a driveby on Broadway."

"What, you like them? You can have mine."

"Naw, why you have to get fresh, Light?" He leaned over and slapped Don again, but lightly. It was the same slap Don had used on Douglas, exactly the same. Don was a reflexive mimic. "You disappoint me."

Don didn't speak.

"What does it want?" said Randall.

"I don't know."

Randall made a face. "I can't get rid of the sucker. It wants me to stop–stop livin' the life?"

"I said I don't know."

"Because I'm not a *user*, Light, I'm not like you. What's it trying to say to me?" Randall lurched forward and Don flinched. Intimidation, I sensed, was a way of life for Randall. It even leaked into interactions where he wanted to propagate trust. He couldn't help it.

"Nothing," said Don.

Randall turned and paced in a tight, impatient circle. "I wanna know, Light. Why this thing in my life, what the *meaning* is. Tell me."

It occurred to me that Randall thought Don knew because he was *white*.

"Nothing."

"Must want something, everybody wants something, Light. It stop you from using?"

"It doesn't give a shit, Randall. It smokes rock. It's a party animal, man."

"Gonna turn me in? Working for the Narcotics?"

"Sure, I don't know. This is fuckin' stupid, Randall."

Randall wheeled. "What you sayin'? It's gathering *evidence*, man? Tell me what you know!"

Kaz and Drey shifted nervously. The gun man cleared his throat.

"Nothing, Randall, man. It can't fuckin' talk, it's from another *planet*, man. Can't turn you in. Relax. It's really got you rattled, man."

"So tell me what it wants."

"Nothing. It's just . . . trying to, you know, get along." Don sighed. "Really, Randall. Everybody wants it to be *about* something, or up *to* something, but it's just, like . . . *attracted*. All the explanations are bullshit."

"That's not right," I blurted. "It's like a guardian angel. It's drawn to you because it senses something—"

I hesitated, and saw that I had everyone's undivided attention.

"—because it feels this sense that you're, uh, *important*, your life is important, and so it's drawn to you." I was going in circles. "It's not *judging* you, it's not moralistic. That's why it doesn't try to stop you, try to change your behavior, why it'll even share the pipe. Drugs aren't the point, it's not some simplistic thing like they make it out to be, it's more subtle than that. It wants to be around you and protect you because—your life is important. And it's afraid that you don't—care enough. So it's trying to do that, to *care*—"

I wanted to convince them, somehow, because I wanted to convince myself.

While I was talking, Don's Sufferer had crept in, like some kind of affirmation of my words. It padded past Don and Randall, stopping a foot or so away from Randall's Sufferer. I stopped talking. The two aliens stared at each other, and the distance between them suddenly seemed very small.

I thought of the aliens' incredible strength. I wished Don's was bigger than Randall's, instead of the reverse.

"Guardian angel," mused Randall. "That your guardian angel, Light?" The sneer in his voice made me sorry I'd spoken at all.

"Yeah," said Don. "It'll always be with you now, Randall. Gonna live your life with you, see everything you do."

"Fuck you trying to say?"

"Nothing. Just that you gotta live right, now, Randall. You're being watched." Don wasn't saying it because it meant anything to him. He was just yanking Randall's chain.

"Huh." Randall thought this over. "Light, you don't know shit about shit. You don't know what I do, how I live."

"Maybe not, Randall."

"I gotta get my money back, Light. Drey, take the money off Light."

Don handed it over, preemptively. I thought of the gun.

"I gotta put a hurt on you, Light, like you put on me. How'm I gonna do that?"

"I dunno."

"What you got that I can take? You ain't got nothing."

The Sufferers suddenly both stood, and I braced for some kind of violence between them. Instead they turned and walked out of the garage together, into the frame of moonlight, and then disappeared around the corner, heading towards the water. To settle their differences?

With them gone I felt naked, doomed.

"Kaz," said Randall, "you gotta do my hurtin' for me, my man. For what Light did to you."

"Naw, Randall," whined Kaz. "Naw, man."

"Hit him."

109

"Naw. He still got a gun, Randall, anyway. You didn't take it off him."

"So take it off him." Randall pointed at me. "You go, chump. You got lucky. Don't fuck with me no more. Don't go around with this dude Light, he's bad news. Go."

"What?" I said.

"Get lost. I ain't gonna fuck with you. You didn't know what you was doing."

"We'll go together," I said. "He's, uh, my brother."

"Go." Randall pointed, and the driver raised the gun at me.

"Go ahead, Paul," said Don.

"No, I'm his brother," I said, getting hysterical. "No."

Randall shoved me towards the door, and the driver followed. I took a few steps.

"Take him, Kaz," commanded Randall, done with me. "Take his gun."

"Naw, don't make me, Randall."

"Do it!"

"I'm his *brother*—"

The driver kicked me, and aimed the gun at my stomach. Inside, Kaz was advancing sheepishly on Don.

I ran, into the glare of moonlight.

Where was the Sufferer? I ran towards the water. Behind me, the clatter of voices: Don, Randall, Kaz. I ran, gasping.

When I found the Sufferers I thought they were killing each other. They were half hidden behind a pile of shredded, stinking tires, in a puddle of stagnant water streaked with oil rainbows. They lay entwined, limbs twisted together, both moaning like echoing wells, their bodies twitching, paws treading air, ears wrinkled back.

Fucking. Making love—the moment it hit me was the moment I heard the shot.

I turned in time to see the four shadows sprinting for the truck. Kaz's voice: "You made me, you made me, you shouldn't of fuckin' made me—"

They'd driven off before I got back to Don.

He was lying on the floor scrabbling in the glass with a hand already sticky with blood. In the dark the blood looked black, and watching it seep out of his stomach was like watching his white sweatshirt disappear into the gloom. It was happening fast.

"Fuck, Paul," he said, when he saw me.

"I'm going to get help," I said.

"Wait, don't leave me—"

"I'll be back—"

I ran out, back under the freeway, and found a woman walking her dog in the park. "For God's sake, my brother got shot, down in the old garage down there, please can you call an ambulance, please—" I fumbled it out between gasps, repeated everything, pointing, and when she agreed I turned and ran back, clutching a knot in my side; a cramp from running, but it felt like a sympathetic wound.

Moving too fast, I slid in his blood, and my knees buckled at seeing how little of the white of the sweatshirt was left. I sat down, in blood and glass, and held his hand.

His gun lay to one side, and I felt suddenly sure that he'd been shot with his own gun, Kaz trying to take it from him. The gun we could have left behind so many times in so many different places.

"I can't see you, man," said Don.

"Your eyes?" My voice was trembling, on the verge of sobs.

"No, stupid, I mean move around here, don't sit behind me."

I shifted. "An ambulance is coming, okay, Donnie? So just

hang on. Guess you'll have to talk to the police or something, huh?"

An hour ago I was still picturing Don in California. Now the dream of seeing him in a hospital bed seemed maybe too much to dare hope for.

"You're so stupid about the cops, Paul." His voice was husky, and as he went on, it got rougher and softer. "I don't care about the cops. When they arrested me before I told the guy 'Thank you, you saved me.' 'Cause I was a skeleton, I weighed about ninety pounds, and I knew I would dry out, get healthy in jail. That's all jail is, man, guys gettin' fed, getting healthy again, doing pushups, so they can go out and do it again. Shit, if they'd given me time instead of parole I might be off rock now."

I started weeping.

"C'mon, Paul, relax."

"We could be on a plane right now," I said. "We were right there, we were at the airport. The Sufferer, the Sufferer ruined everything."

"Nah, man, I didn't want to go. Tony the Tiger didn't blow it."

"Why? Why couldn't we just go?"

"I was all freaked out. I mean, it sounds great, right? Start over, cut out, leave all the shit behind. But I wasn't ready. I was just going along, I didn't want to disappoint you."

"What do you mean?"

"If California is my big second chance, Paul, I don't wanna go fuck it up with my pockets full of rock. I wanted it to be like you said, but I wasn't ready, I was afraid. If I went and I was still all fucked up there—I didn't want to disappoint you, Paul. At least if we didn't go I hadn't fucked up *California*. It was still there, like this beautiful picture you were painting, you know—"

His voice was trailing off, and I could barely hear him for my own sobbing.

"It was sort of hard for me to think about California or whatever, anything else, with all that rock in my coat, Paul. When we took Kaz for rock instead of cash . . . I had to get rid of it, and if I had to get rid of it, why not get high, you know? You don't know . . . you don't know how much I . . . like to get *high*, Paul. You haven't been *around* me that much. We haven't been in touch. I'm not just, like, the little kid you knew. I been . . . *doing* stuff—"

"My fault, the whole thing about robbing Kaz. You did that because of my stupid idea, to get cash for the tickets."

"Yeah, yeah, let's blame it all on you and the monster. Whatever. But the California thing . . . wasn't stupid. It was a good idea, so relax now, okay?"

"Okay."

"Shut up now and stop making me talk so much, right?"

"Okay."

"We'll go . . . we'll still go to California."

I didn't say anything, and Don closed his eyes, and we were quiet. The pace of blood leaking through his shirt slowed down. Time seemed to slow with it.

"I'm gonna pass out now," he said.

"Okay," I managed.

"I'm just . . . passing out, right, I'm not *dying*."

He couldn't see his sweatshirt. "Right," I said.

He was dead for almost five minutes before I finally heard sirens, and they weren't even close yet.

I made a quick calculation about talking to a long series of people about what happened, starting with the ambulance people and the police and ending with our parents, versus getting the hell out of there. It wasn't a hard call.

I took Don's pipe and lighter and put them in my pocket

and ran, south under the highway, and circled around a couple of blocks back to Broadway.

I hopped the turnstile and took the IRT downtown, to the Village, then walked across West 3rd Street to Washington Square Park, where life went on as usual, all night every night, every night for the last thirty years, probably. I sat on the same bench I'd been on at noon, waiting for Don to turn up, finding him after so long. Now I had to share it with a guy who was sleeping, but his smell and my stare kept anyone else away.

I wondered if I was waiting for Kaz. I couldn't think of what I would do or say if he showed, so I guessed I wasn't.

I started feeling sleepy about the same time the sky began to lighten up. The deadest hour in the park, when the night is officially over. A few businessmen walked across, and joggers. It was their park now, for a few short hours.

I got off my bench and managed to find someone dealing. There's always someone dealing. If I'd said to him: "You seen Kaz?" or "You seen Light?" he probably would have said: "Naw, man. But he be around later. What you want him for?"

Instead I just scored a five-dollar vial and went back to my bench.

I put it into Don's pipe and flickered the lighter over it and drew a hit, and at that moment the Sufferer walked up. It sat down in front of me and cocked its head.

I tried to ignore it, which worked for about five seconds. Then, riding the rush from the crack, I jumped on it and started beating its face with my fists. "You didn't do anything!" I screamed. The Sufferer just twisted slowly away from my blows, squinting its big eyes, shifting its feet to accommodate my assault. "You didn't help him at all! You didn't change anything!"

A crowd began to gather around us. "You were fucking, you were fucking when they killed him!" My voice cracked with rage, and I tasted my snot and tears as they ran down my face. I beat at it, my fists aching, then tried to reach for its mouth, its "Achilles tendon," but it just butted me away with its cheek. "You didn't help him at all!"

A couple of Rastafarians came forward out of the crowd and plucked me away. "Easy there, little man, come on. It didn't hurt you now, you just hurting yourself. Easy up."

I squirmed out of their grasp and fell to the pavement in front of the Sufferer. The alien opened its mouth and moaned silently at me, then took a step away from me. The crowd ducked quickly out of its way, though it hadn't made a sudden or violent movement yet.

Sickened, trembling, I crawled off the pavement, into the grassy section behind the benches.

Soon enough the little knot of attention that had gathered around us was dissolved back into the park. The Sufferer wandered away too.

When the trembling passed I got up and staggered out of the park, half blind with hunger and exhaustion. The Village swirled around me, oblivious. I thought about Don weighing ninety pounds, reaching the end of his run, thanking the cops for taking him off the street, for noticing him at all.

I don't know how long I walked before I passed out on the bench on Sixth Avenue, in front of the basketball courts, but when I woke again, the sun was low. People were going home from work. I was freezing. The Sufferer was staring at me, its face inches from mine.

I reached out, weak, wanting to hit it or twist its ears and to take its warmth at the same time.

It pulled away, and turned and trotted down Sixth. "You

fucker," I said. "It would have been better if you'd never come at all."

I could have been talking to myself. Maybe I was.

I watched the Sufferer turn the corner, and I never saw it again after that.

The Brooklyn Bridge has a walkway. The Manhattan used to, but doesn't anymore. I crossed the bridge under an orange sky. I walked through downtown Brooklyn to Flatbush Avenue, and took the Long Island Railroad to Plainview, to tell Jimmy and Marilla that I knew what had happened to Don, to Donovan, to Light.

How We Got in Town and out Again

When we first saw somebody near the mall Gloria and I looked around for sticks. We were going to rob them if they were few enough. The mall was about five miles out of the town we were headed for, so nobody would know. But when we got closer Gloria saw their vans and said they were scapers. I didn't know what that was, but she told me.

It was summer. Two days before this Gloria and I had broken out of a pack of people that had food but we couldn't stand their religious chanting anymore. We hadn't eaten since then.

"So what do we do?" I said.

"You let me talk," said Gloria.

"You think we could get into town with them?"

"Better than that," she said. "Just keep quiet."

I dropped the piece of pipe I'd found and we walked in across the parking lot. This mall was long past being good for finding food anymore but the scapers were taking out folding chairs from a store and strapping them on top of their vans. There were four men and one woman.

"Hey," said Gloria.

Two guys were just lugs and they ignored us and kept lugging. The woman was sitting in the front of the van. She was smoking a cigarette.

The other two guys turned. This was Kromer and Fearing, but I didn't know their names yet.

"Beat it," said Kromer. He was a tall squinty guy with a gold tooth. He was kind of worn but the tooth said he'd never lost a fight or slept in a flop. "We're busy," he said.

He was being reasonable. If you weren't in a town you were nowhere. Why talk to someone you met nowhere?

But the other guy smiled at Gloria. He had a thin face and a little mustache. "Who are you?" he said. He didn't look at me.

"I know what you guys do," Gloria said. "I was in one before."

"Oh?" said the guy, still smiling.

"You're going to need contestants," she said.

"She's a fast one," this guy said to the other guy. "I'm Fearing," he said to Gloria.

"Fearing what?" said Gloria.

"Just Fearing."

"Well, I'm just Gloria."

"That's fine," said Fearing. "This is Tommy Kromer. We run this thing. What's your little friend's name?"

"I can say my own name," I said. "I'm Lewis."

"Are you from the lovely town up ahead?"

"Nope," said Gloria. "We're headed there."

"Getting in exactly how?" said Fearing.

"Anyhow," said Gloria, like it was an answer. "With you, now."

"That's assuming something pretty quick."

"Or we could go and say how you ripped off the last town and they sent us to warn about you," said Gloria.

"Fast," said Fearing again, grinning, and Kromer shook his head. They didn't look too worried.

"You ought to want me along," said Gloria. "I'm an attraction."

"Can't hurt," said Fearing. Kromer shrugged, and said, "Skinny, for an attraction."

"Sure, I'm skinny," she said. "That's why me and Lewis ought to get something to eat."

Fearing stared at her. Kromer was back to the van with the other guys.

"Or if you can't feed us—" started Gloria.

"Hold it, sweetheart. No more threats."

"We need a meal."

"We'll eat something when we get in," Fearing said. "You and Lewis can get a meal if you're both planning to enter."

"Sure," she said. "We're gonna enter—right Lewis?"

I knew to say right.

The town militia came out to meet the vans, of course. But they seemed to know the scapers were coming, and after Fearing talked to them for a couple of minutes they opened up the doors and had a quick look then waved us through. Gloria and I were in the back of a van with a bunch of equipment and one of the lugs, named Ed. Kromer drove. Fearing drove the van with the woman in it. The other lug drove the last one alone.

I'd never gotten into a town in a van before, but I'd only gotten in two times before this anyway. The first time by myself, just by creeping in, the second because Gloria went with a militia guy.

Towns weren't so great anyway. Maybe this would be different.

We drove a few blocks and a guy flagged Fearing down. He came up to the window of the van and they talked, then went back to his car, waving at Kromer on his way. Then we followed him.

"What's that about?" said Gloria.

119

"Gilmartin's the advance man," said Kromer. "I thought you knew everything."

Gloria didn't talk. I said, "What's an advance man?"

"Gets us a place, and the juice we need," said Kromer. "Softens the town up. Gets people excited."

It was getting dark. I was pretty hungry, but I didn't say anything. Gilmartin's car led us to this big building shaped like a boathouse only it wasn't near any water. Kromer said it used to be a bowling alley.

The lugs started moving stuff and Kromer made me help. The building was dusty and empty inside, and some of the lights didn't work. Kromer said just to get things inside for now. He drove away one of the vans and came back and we unloaded a bunch of little cots that Gilmartin the advance man had rented, so I had an idea where I was going to be sleeping. Apart from that it was stuff for the contest. Computer cables and plastic spacesuits, and loads of televisions.

Fearing took Gloria and they came back with food, fried chicken and potato salad, and we all ate. I couldn't stop going back for more but nobody said anything. Then I went to sleep on a cot. No one was talking to me. Gloria wasn't sleeping on a cot. I think she was with Fearing.

Gilmartin the advance man had really done his work. The town was sniffing around first thing in the morning. Fearing was out talking to them when I woke up. "Registration begins at noon, not a minute sooner," he was saying. "Beat the lines and stick around. We'll be serving coffee. Be warned, only the fit need apply—our doctor will be examining you, and he's never been fooled once. It's Darwinian logic, people. The future is for the strong. The meek will have to inherit the here and now."

Inside, Ed and the other guy were setting up the gear.

They had about thirty of those wired-up plastic suits stretched out in the middle of the place, and so tangled up with cable and little wires that they were like husks of fly bodies in a spiderweb.

Under each of the suits was a light metal frame, sort of like a bicycle with a seat but no wheels, but with a headrest too. Around the web they were setting up the televisions in an arc facing the seats. The suits each had a number on the back, and the televisions had numbers on top that matched.

When Gloria turned up she didn't say anything to me but she handed me some donuts and coffee.

"This is just the start," she said, when she saw my eyes get big. "We're in for three squares a day as long as this thing lasts. As long as we last, anyway."

We sat and ate outside where we could listen to Fearing. He went on and on. Some people were lined up like he said. I didn't blame them since Fearing was such a talker. Others listened and just got nervous or excited and went away, but I could tell they were coming back later, at least to watch. When we finished the donuts Fearing came over and told us to get on line too.

"We don't have to," said Gloria.

"Yes, you do," said Fearing.

On line we met Lane. She said she was twenty like Gloria but she looked younger. She could have been sixteen, like me.

"You ever do this before?" asked Gloria.

Lane shook her head. "You?"

"Sure," said Gloria. "You ever been out of this town?"

"A couple of times," said Lane. "When I was a kid. I'd like to now."

"Why?"

"I broke up with my boyfriend."

Gloria stuck out her lip, and said. "But you're scared to leave town, so you're doing this instead."

Lane shrugged.

I liked her, but Gloria didn't.

The doctor turned out to be Gilmartin the advance man. I don't think he was a real doctor, but he listened to my heart. Nobody ever did that before, and it gave me a good feeling.

Registration was a joke, though. It was for show. They asked a lot of questions but they only sent a couple of women and one guy away, Gloria said for being too old. Everyone else was okay, despite how some of them looked pretty hungry, just like me and Gloria. This was a hungry town. Later I figured out that's part of why Fearing and Kromer picked it. You'd think they'd want to go where the money was, but you'd be wrong.

After registration they told us to get lost for the afternoon. Everything started at eight o'clock.

We walked around downtown but almost all the shops were closed. All the good stuff was in the shopping center and you had to show a town ID card to get in and me and Gloria didn't have those.

So, like Gloria always says, we killed time since time was what we had.

The place looked different. They had spotlights pointed from on top of the vans and Fearing was talking through a microphone. There was a banner up over the doors. I asked Gloria and she said "Scape-Athon." Ed was selling beer out of a cooler and some people were buying, even though he must have just bought it right there in town for half the price he was selling at. It was a hot night. They were selling tickets but they weren't letting anybody in yet. Fearing told us to get inside.

Most of the contestants were there already. Anne, the woman from the van, was there, acting like any other contestant. Lane was there too and we waved at each other. Gilmartin was helping everybody put on the suits. You had to get naked but nobody seemed to mind. Just being contestants made it all right, like we were invisible to each other.

"Can we be next to each other?" I said to Gloria.

"Sure, except it doesn't matter," she said. "We won't be able to see each other inside."

"Inside where?" I said.

"The scapes," she said. "You'll see."

Gloria got me into my suit. It was plastic with wiring everywhere and padding at my knees and wrists and elbows and under my arms and in my crotch. I tried on the mask but it was heavy and I saw nobody else was wearing theirs so I kept it off until I had to. Then Gilmartin tried to help Gloria but she said she could do it herself.

So there we were, standing around half naked and dripping with cable in the big empty lit up bowling alley, and then suddenly Fearing and his big voice came inside and they let the people in and the lights went down and it all started.

"Thirty-two young souls ready to swim out of this world, into the bright shiny future," went Fearing. "The question is, how far into that future will their bodies take them? New worlds are theirs for the taking—a cornucopia of scapes to boggle and amaze and gratify the senses. These lucky kids will be immersed in an ocean of data overwhelming to their undernourished sensibilities—we've assembled a really brilliant collection of environments for them to explore—

and you'll be able to see everything they see, on the monitors in front of you. But can they make it in the fast lane? How long can they ride the wave? Which of them will prove able to outlast the others, and take home the big prize—one thousand dollars? That's what we're here to find out."

Gilmartin and Ed were snapping everybody into their masks and turning all the switches to wire us up and getting us to lie down on the frames. It was comfortable on the bicycle seat with your head on the headrest and a belt around your waist. You could move your arms and legs like you were swimming, the way Fearing said. I didn't mind putting on the mask now because the audience was making me nervous. A lot of them I couldn't see because of the lights, but I could tell they were there, watching.

The mask covered my ears and eyes. Around my chin there was a strip of wire and tape. Inside it was dark and quiet at first except Fearing's voice was still coming into the earphones.

"The rules are simple. Our contestants get a thirty minute rest period every three hours. These kids'll be well fed, don't worry about that. Our doctor will monitor their health. You've heard the horror stories, but we're a class outfit; you'll see no horrors here. The kids earn the quality care we provide one way: continuous, waking engagement with the datastream. We're firm on that. To sleep is to die—you can sleep on your own time, but not ours. One lapse, and you're out of the game—them's the rules."

The earphones started to hum. I wished I could reach out and hold Gloria's hand, but she was too far away.

"They'll have no help from the floor judges, or one another, in locating the perceptual riches of cyberspace. Some will discover the keys that open the doors to a thousand worlds, others will bog down in the antechamber to the future. Anyone caught coaching during rest periods will be disqualified—no warnings, no second chances."

Then Fearing's voice dropped out, and the scapes started.

I was in a hallway. The walls were full of drawers, like a big cabinet that went on forever. The drawers had writing on them that I ignored. First I couldn't move except my head, then I figured out how to walk, and just did that for a while. But I never got anywhere. It felt like I was walking in a giant circle, up the wall, across the ceiling, and then back down the other wall.

So I pulled open a drawer. It only looked big enough to hold some pencils or whatever but when I pulled it opened like a door and I went through.

"Welcome to Intense Personals," said a voice. There was just some colors to look at. The door closed behind me. "You must be eighteen years of age or older to use this service. To avoid any charges, please exit now."

I didn't exit because I didn't know how. The space with colors was kind of small except it didn't have any edges. But it felt small.

"This is the main menu. Please reach out and make one of the following selections: women seeking men, men seeking women, women seeking women, men seeking men, or alternatives."

Each of them was a block of words in the air. I reached up and touched the first one.

"After each selection touch *one* to play the recording again, *two* to record a message for this person, or *three* to advance to the next selection. You may touch three at any time to advance to the next selection, or four to return to the main menu."

Then a woman came into the colored space with me. She was dressed up and wearing lipstick.

"Hi, my name is Kate," she said. She stared like she was looking through my head at something behind me, and poked at her hair while she talked. "I live in San Francisco. I work in the financial district, as a personnel manager, but my real love is the arts, currently painting and writing—"

"How did you get into San Francisco?" I said.

"—just bought a new pair of hiking boots and I'm hoping to tackle Mount Tam this weekend," she said, ignoring me.

"I never met anyone from there," I said.

"—looking for a man who's not intimidated by intelligence," she went on. "It's important that you like what you do, like where you are. I also want someone who's confident enough that I can express my vulnerability. You should be a good listener—"

I touched three. I can read numbers.

Another woman came in, just like that. This one was as young as Gloria, but kind of soft-looking.

"I continue to ask myself why in the *heck* I'm doing this personals thing," she said, sighing. "But I know the reason—I want to date. I'm new to the San Francisco area. I like to go to the theater, but I'm really open-minded. I was born and raised in Chicago, so I think I'm a little more east coast than west. I'm fast-talking and cynical. I guess I'm getting a little cynical about these ads, the sky has yet to part, lightning has yet to strike—"

I got rid of her, now that I knew how.

"—I have my own garden and landscape business—"

"—someone who's fun, not nerdy—"

"—I'm tender, I'm sensuous—"

I started to wonder how long ago these women were from. I didn't like the way they were making me feel, sort of guilty and bullied at the same time. I didn't think I could make any of them happy the way they were hoping but I didn't think I was going to get a chance to try, anyway.

It took pretty long for me to get back out into the hallway. From then on I paid more attention to how I got into things.

The next drawer I got into was just about the opposite. All space and no people. I was driving an airplane over almost the whole world, as far as I could tell. There was a row of dials and switches under the windows but it didn't mean anything to me. First I was in the mountains and I crashed a lot, and that was dull because a voice would lecture me before I could start again, and I had to wait. But then I got to the desert and I kept it up without crashing much. I just learned to say "no" whenever the voice suggested something different like "engage target" or "evasive action." I wanted to fly a while, that's all. The desert looked good from up there, even though I'd been walking around in deserts too often.

Except that I had to pee I could have done that forever. Fearing's voice broke in, though, and said it was time for the first rest period.

"—still fresh and eager after their first plunge into the wonders of the future," Fearing was saying to the people in the seats. The place was only half full. "Already this world seems drab by comparison. Yet, consider the irony, that as their questing minds grow accustomed to these splendors, their bodies will begin to rebel—"

Gloria showed me how to unsnap the cables so I could walk out of the middle of all that stuff still wearing the suit, leaving the mask behind. Everybody lined up for the bathroom. Then we went to the big hall in the back where they had the cots, but nobody went to sleep or anything. I guessed we'd all want to next time, but right now I was too excited and so was everybody else. Fearing just kept talking like us taking a break was as much a part of the show as anything else.

"Splendors, hah," said Gloria. "Bunch of second-hand cyber junk."

"I was in a plane," I started.

"Shut up," said Gloria. "We're not supposed to talk about it. Only, if you find something you like, remember where it is."

I hadn't done that, but I wasn't worried.

"Drink some water," she said. "And get some food."

They were going around with sandwiches and I got a couple, one for Gloria. But she didn't seem to want to talk.

Gilmartin the fake doctor was making a big deal of going around checking everybody even though it was only the first break. I figured that the whole point of taking care of us so hard was to remind the people in the seats that they might see somebody get hurt.

Ed was giving out apples from a bag. I took one and went over and sat on Lane's cot. She looked nice in her suit.

"My boyfriend's here," she said.

"You're back together?"

"I mean ex-. I'm pretending I didn't see him."

"Where?"

"He's sitting right in front of my monitor." She tipped her head to point.

I didn't say anything but I wished I had somebody watching me from the audience.

When I went back the first thing I got into was a library of books. Every one you took off the shelf turned into a show, with charts and pictures, but when I figured out that it was all business stuff about how to manage your money, I got bored.

Then I went into a dungeon. It started with a wizard growing me up from a bug. We were in his workshop, which was all full of jars and cobwebs. He had a face like a melted candle and he talked as much as Fearing. There were bats flying around.

"You must resume the quest of Kroyd," he said to me, and started touching me with his stick. I could see my arms and legs, but they weren't wearing the scaper suit. They were covered with muscles. When the wizard touched me I got a sword and a shield. "These are your companions, Rip and Batter," said the wizard. "They will obey you and protect you. You must never betray them for any other. That was Kroyd's mistake."

"Okay," I said.

The wizard sent me into the dungeon and Rip and Batter talked to me. They told me what to do. They sounded a lot like the wizard.

We met a Wormlion. That's what Rip and Batter called it. It had a head full of worms with little faces and Rip and Batter said to kill it, which wasn't hard. The head exploded and all the worms started running away into the stones of the floor like water.

Then we met a woman in sexy clothes who was holding a sword and shield too. Hers were loaded with jewels and looked a lot nicer than Rip and Batter. This was Kroyd's mistake, anyone could see that. Only I figured Kroyd wasn't here and I was, and so maybe his mistake was one I wanted to make too.

Rip and Batter started screaming when I traded with the woman, and then she put them on and we fought. When she killed me I was back in the doorway to the Wizard's room, where I first ran in, bug-sized. This time I went the other way, back to the drawers.

Which is when I met the snowman.

I was looking around in a drawer that didn't seem to have anything in it. Everything was just black. Then I saw a little blinking list of numbers in the corner. I touched the numbers. None of them did anything except one.

It was still black but there were five pictures of a snowman. He was three balls of white, more like plastic than snow. His eyes were just o's and his mouth didn't move right when he talked. His arms were sticks but they bent like rubber. There were two pictures of him small and far away, one from underneath like he was on a hill and one that showed the top of his head, like he was in a hole. Then there was a big one of just his head, and a big one of his whole body. The last one was of him looking in through a window, only you couldn't see the window, just the way it cut off part of the snowman.

"What's your name?" he said.

"Lewis."

"I'm Mr. Sneeze." His head and arms moved in all five pictures when he talked. His eyes got big and small.

"What's this place you're in?"

"It's no place," said Mr. Sneeze. "Just a garbage file."

"Why do you live in a garbage file?"

"Copyright lawyers," said Mr. Sneeze. "I made them nervous." He sounded happy no matter what he was saying.

"Nervous about what?"

"I was in a Christmas special for interactive television. But at the last minute somebody from the legal department thought I looked too much like a snowman on a video game called *Mud Flinger*. It was too late to redesign me so they just cut me out and dumped me in this file."

"Can't you go somewhere else?"

"I don't have too much mobility." He jumped and twirled upside down and landed in the same place, five times at once. The one without a body spun too.

"Do you miss the show?"

"I just hope they're doing well. Everybody has been working so hard."

I didn't want to tell him it was probably a long time ago.

"What are you doing here, Lewis?" said Mr. Sneeze.

"I'm in a scape-athon."

"What's that?"

I told him about Gloria and Fearing and Kromer, and about the contest. I think he liked that he was on television again.

There weren't too many people left in the seats. Fearing was talking to them about what was going to happen tomorrow when they came back. Kromer and Ed got us all in the back. I looked over at Lane's cot. She was already asleep. Her boyfriend was gone from the chair out front.

I lay down on the cot beside Gloria. "I'm tired now," I said.

"So sleep a little," she said, and put her arm over me. But I could hear Fearing outside talking about a "Sexathon" and I asked Gloria what it was.

"That's tomorrow night," she said. "Don't worry about it now."

Gloria wasn't going to sleep, just looking around.

I found the SmartHouse Showroom. It was a house with a voice inside. At first I was looking around to see who the voice was but then I figured out it was the house.

"Answer the phone!" it said. The phone was ringing.

I picked up the phone, and the lights in the room changed to a desk light on the table with the phone. The music in the room turned off.

"How's that for responsiveness?"

"Fine," I said. I hung up the phone. There was a television in the room, and it turned on. It was a picture of food. "See that?"

"The food, you mean?" I said.

"That's the contents of your refrigerator!" it said. "The packages with the blue halo will go bad in the next twenty-four hours. The package with the black halo has already expired! Would you like me to dispose of it for you?"

"Sure."

"Now look out the windows!"

I looked. There were mountains outside.

"Imagine waking up in the Alps every morning!"

"I—"

"And when you're ready for work, your car is already warm in the garage!"

The windows switched from the mountains to a picture of a car in a garage.

"And your voicemail tells callers that you're not home when it senses the car is gone from the garage!"

I wondered if there was somewhere I could get if I went down to drive the car. But they were trying to sell me this house, so probably not.

"And the television notifies you when the book you're reading is available this week as a movie!"

The television switched to a movie, the window curtains closed, and the light by the phone went off.

"I can't read," I said.

"All the more important, then, isn't it?" said the house.

"What about the bedroom?" I said. I was thinking about sleep.

"Here you go!" A door opened and I went in. The bedroom had another television. But the bed wasn't right. It had a scribble of electronic stuff over it.

"What's wrong with the bed?"

"Somebody defaced it," said the house. "Pity."

I knew it must have been Fearing or Kromer who wrecked the bed because they didn't want anyone getting that comfortable and falling asleep and out of the contest. At least not yet.

"Sorry!" said the house. "Let me show you the work center!"

Next rest I got right into Gloria's cot and curled up and she curled around me. It was real early in the morning and nobody was watching the show now and Fearing wasn't talking. I think he was off taking a nap of his own.

Kromer woke us up. "He always have to sleep with you, like a baby?"

Gloria said, "Leave him alone. He can sleep where he wants."

"I can't figure," said Kromer. "Is he your boyfriend or your kid brother?"

"Neither," said Gloria. "What do you care?"

"Okay," said Kromer. "We've got a job for him to do tomorrow, though."

"What job?" said Gloria. They talked like I wasn't there.

"We need a hacker boy for a little sideshow we put on," said Kromer. "He's it."

"He's never been in a scape before," said Gloria. "He's no hacker."

"He's the nearest we've got. We'll walk him through it."

"I'll do it," I said.

"Okay, but then leave him out of the Sexathon," said Gloria.

Kromer smiled. "You're protecting him? Sorry. Everybody plays in the Sexathon, sweetheart. That's bread and butter. The customers don't let us break the rules." He pointed out to the rigs. "You'd better get out there."

I knew Kromer thought I didn't know about Gloria and Fearing, or other things. I wanted to tell him I wasn't so innocent, but I didn't think Gloria would like it, so I kept quiet.

I went to talk to Mr. Sneeze. I remembered where he was from the first time.

"What's a Sexathon?" I said.

"I don't know, Lewis."

"I've never had sex," I said.

"Me neither," said Mr. Sneeze.

"Everybody always thinks I do with Gloria just because we go around together. But we're just friends."

"That's fine," said Mr. Sneeze. "It's okay to be friends."

"I'd like to be Lane's boyfriend," I said.

Next break Gloria slept while Gilmartin and Kromer told me about the act. A drawer would be marked for me to go into, and there would be a lot of numbers and letters but I just had to keep pressing "1–2–3" no matter what. It was supposed to be a security archive, they said. The people watching would think I was breaking codes but it was just for show. Then something else would happen but they wouldn't say what, just that I should keep quiet and let Fearing talk. So I knew they were going to pull me out of my mask. I didn't know if I should tell Gloria.

Fearing was up again welcoming some people back in. I couldn't believe anybody wanted to start watching first thing in the morning but Fearing was saying "the gritty determination to survive that epitomizes the frontier spirit that once made a country called America great" and "young bodies writhing in agonized congress with the future" and that sounded like a lot of fun, I guess.

A woman from the town had quit already. Not Lane though.

A good quiet place to go was Mars. It was like the airplane, all space and no people, but better since there was no voice telling you to engage targets, and you never crashed.

I went to the drawer they told me about. Fearing's voice in my ear told me it was time. The place was a storeroom of information like the business library. No people, just files with a lot of blinking lights and complicated words. A voice kept asking me for "security clearance password" but there was always a place for me to touch "1–2–3" and I did. It was kind of a joke, like a wall made out of feathers that falls apart every time you touch it.

I found a bunch of papers with writing. Some of the words were blacked out and some were bright red and blinking. There was a siren sound. Then I felt hands pulling on me from outside and somebody took off my mask.

There were two guys pulling on me who I had never seen before, and Ed and Kromer were pulling on them. Everybody was screaming at each other but it was kind of fake, because nobody was pulling or yelling very hard. Fearing said "The feds, the feds!" A bunch of people were crowded around my television screen I guess looking at the papers I'd dug up, but now they were watching the action.

Fearing came over and pulled out a toy gun and so did Kromer, and they were backing the two men away from me. I'm sure the audience could tell it was fake. But they were pretty excited, maybe just from remembering when feds were real.

I got off my frame and looked around. I didn't know what they were going to do with me now that I was out but I didn't care. It was my first chance to see what it was like when the contestants were all in their suits and masks, swimming in the information. None of them knew what was happening, not even Gloria, who was right next to me the whole time. They just kept moving in the scapes. I looked at Lane. She looked good, like she was dancing.

Meanwhile Fearing and Kromer chased those guys out the back. People were craning around to see. Fearing came out and took his microphone and said, "It isn't his fault, folks. Just good hacker instincts for ferreting out corruption from encrypted data. The feds don't want us digging up their trail, but the kid couldn't help it."

Ed and Kromer started snapping me back into my suit. "We chased them off," Fearing said, patting his gun. "We do take care of our own. You can't tell who's going to come sniffing around, can you? For his protection and ours we're going to have to delete that file, but it goes to show, there's no limit to what a kid with a nose for data's going to root out of cyberspace. We can't throw him out of the contest for doing what comes natural. Give him a big hand, folks."

People clapped and a few threw coins. Ed picked the change up for me, then told me to put on my mask. Meanwhile Gloria and Lane and everybody else just went on through their scapes.

I began to see what Kromer and Fearing were selling. It

wasn't any one thing. Some of it was fake and some was real, and some was a mix so you couldn't tell.

The people watching probably didn't know why they wanted to, except it made them forget their screwed-up life for a while to watch the only suckers bigger than themselves—us.

"Meanwhile, the big show goes on," said Fearing. "How long will they last? Who will take the prize?"

I told Gloria about it at the break. She just shrugged and said to make sure I got my money from Kromer. Fearing was talking to Anne the woman from the van and Gloria was staring at them like she wanted them dead.

A guy was lying in his cot talking to himself as if nobody could hear and Gilmartin and Kromer went over and told him he was kicked out. He didn't seem to care.

I went to see Lane but we didn't talk. We sat on her cot and held hands. I didn't know if it meant the same thing to her that it did to me but I liked it.

After the break I went and talked to Mr. Sneeze. He told me the story of the show about Christmas. He said it wasn't about always getting gifts. Sometimes you had to give gifts too.

The Sexathon was late at night. They cleared the seats and everyone had to pay again to get back in, because it was a special event. Fearing had built it up all day, talking about how it was for adults only, it would separate the men from the boys, things like that. Also that people would get knocked out of the contest. So we were pretty nervous by the time he told us the rules.

"What would scapes be without virtual sex?" he said. "Our voyageurs must now prove themselves in the sensual realm—for the future consists of far more than cold, hard information. It's a place of desire and temptation, and, as always, survival belongs to the fittest. The soldiers will now be steered onto the sexual battlescape—the question is, will they meet with the Little Death, or the Big one?"

Gloria wouldn't explain. "Not real death," is all she said.

"The rules again are so simple a child could follow them. In the Sex-Scape environment our contestants will be free to pick from a variety of fantasy partners. We've packed this program with options, there's something for every taste, believe you me. We won't question their selections, but— here's the catch—we will chart the results. Their suits will tell us who does and doesn't attain sexual orgasm in the next session, and those who don't will be handed their walking papers. The suits don't lie. Find bliss or die, folks, find bliss or die."

"You get it now?" said Gloria to me.

"I guess," I said.

"As ever, audience members are cautioned never to inter-fere with the contestants during play. Follow their fantasies on the monitors, or watch their youthful bodies strain against exhaustion, seeking to bridge virtual lust and bona fide physical response. But no touchee."

Kromer was going around, checking the suits. "Who's gonna be in your fantasy, kid?" he said to me. "The snowman?"

I'd forgotten how they could watch me talk to Mr. Sneeze on my television. I turned red.

"Screw you, Kromer," said Gloria.

"Whoever you want, honey," he said, laughing.

Well I found my way around their Sex-Scape and I'm not too embarrassed to say I found a girl who reminded me of

Lane, except for the way she was trying so hard to be sexy. But she looked like Lane. I didn't have to do much to get the subject around to sex. It was the only thing on her mind. She wanted me to tell her what I wanted to do to her and when I couldn't think of much she suggested things and I just agreed. And when I did that she would move around and sigh as if it were really exciting to talk about even though she was doing the talking. She wanted to touch me but she couldn't really so she took off her clothes and got close to me and touched herself. I touched her too but she didn't really feel like much and it was like my hands were made of wood, which couldn't have felt too nice for her though she acted like it was great.

I touched myself a little too. I tried not to think about the audience. I was a little confused about what was what in the suit and with her breathing in my ear so loud but I got the desired result. That wasn't hard for me.

Then I could go back to the drawers but Kromer had made me embarrassed about visiting Mr. Sneeze so I went to Mars even though I would have liked to talk to him.

The audience was all stirred up at the next break. They were sure getting their money's worth now. I got into Gloria's cot. I asked her if she did it with her own hands too. "You didn't have to do that," she said.

"How else?"

"I just pretended. I don't think they can tell. They just want to see you wiggle around."

Well some of the women from the town hadn't wiggled around enough I guess because Kromer and Ed were taking them out of the contest. A couple of them were crying.

"I wish I hadn't," I said.

"It's the same either way," said Gloria. "Don't feel bad. Probably some other people did it too."

They didn't kick Lane out but I saw she was crying anyway.

Kromer brought a man into the back and said to me, "Get into your own cot, little snowman."

"Let him stay," said Gloria. She wasn't looking at Kromer.

"I've got someone here who wants to meet you," said Kromer to Gloria. "Mr. Warren, this is Gloria."

Mr. Warren shook her hand. He was pretty old. "I've been admiring you," he said. "You're very good."

"Mr. Warren is wondering if you'd let him buy you a drink," said Kromer.

"Thanks, but I need some sleep," said Gloria.

"Perhaps later," said Mr. Warren.

After he left Kromer came back and said, "You shouldn't pass up easy money."

"I don't need it," said Gloria. "I'm going to win your contest, you goddamn pimp."

"Now, Gloria," said Kromer. "You don't want to give the wrong impression."

"Leave me alone."

I noticed now that Anne wasn't around in the rest area and I got the idea that the kind of easy money Gloria didn't want Anne did. I'm not so dumb.

Worrying about the Sexathon had stopped me from feeling how tired I was. Right after that I started nodding off in the scapes. I had to keep moving around. After I'd been to a few new things I went to see the snowman again. It was early in the morning and I figured Kromer was probably asleep and there was barely any audience to see what I was doing on my television. So Mr. Sneeze and I talked and that helped me stay awake.

I wasn't the only one who was tired after that night. On the next break I saw that a bunch of people had dropped out or been kicked out for sleeping. There were only seventeen left. I couldn't stay awake myself. But I woke up when I heard some yelling over where Lane was.

It was her parents. I guess they heard about the Sexathon, maybe from her boyfriend, who was there too. Lane was sitting crying behind Fearing who was telling her parents to get out of there, and her father just kept saying "I'm her father! I'm her father!" Her mother was pulling at Fearing but Ed came over and pulled on her.

I started to get up but Gloria grabbed my arm and said, "Stay out of this."

"Lane doesn't want to see that guy," I said.

"Let the townies take care of themselves, Lewis. Let Lane's daddy take her home if he can. Worse could happen to her."

"You just want her out of the contest," I said.

Gloria laughed. "I'm not worried about your girlfriend outlasting me," she said. "She's about to break no matter what."

So I just watched. Kromer and Ed got Lane's parents and boyfriend pushed out of the rest area, back toward the seats. Fearing was yelling at them, making a scene for the audience. It was all part of the show as far as he was concerned.

Anne from the van was over talking to Lane, who was still crying, but quiet now.

"Do you really think you can win?" I said to Gloria.

"Sure, why not?" she said. "I can last."

"I'm pretty tired." In fact my eyeballs felt like they were full of sand.

"Well if you fall out stick around. You can probably get food out of Kromer for cleaning up or something. I'm going to take these bastards."

"You don't like Fearing anymore," I said.

"I never did," said Gloria.

That afternoon three more people dropped out. Fearing was going on about endurance and I got thinking about how much harder it was to live the way me and Gloria did than it was to be in town and so maybe we had an advantage. Maybe that was why Gloria thought she could win now. But I sure didn't feel it myself. I was so messed up that I couldn't always sleep at the rest periods, just lie there and listen to Fearing or eat their sandwiches until I wanted to vomit.

Kromer and Gilmartin were planning some sideshow but it didn't involve me and I didn't care. I didn't want coins thrown at me. I just wanted to get through.

If I built the cities near the water the plague always killed all the people and if I built the cities near the mountains the volcanoes always killed all the people and if I built the cities on the plain the other tribe always came over and killed all the people and I got sick of the whole damn thing.

"When Gloria wins we could live in town for a while," I said. "We could even get jobs if there are any. Then if Lane doesn't want to go back to her parents she could stay with us."

"You could win the contest," said Mr. Sneeze.

"I don't think so," I said. "But Gloria could."

Why did Lewis cross Mars? To get to the other side. Ha ha.

I came out for the rest period and Gloria was already yelling and I unhooked my suit and rushed over to see what was the matter. It was so late it was getting light outside and almost nobody was in the place. "She's cheating!" Gloria screamed. She was pounding on Kromer and he was backing up because she was a handful mad. "That bitch is cheating! You let her sleep!" Gloria pointed at Anne from the van. "She's lying there asleep, you're running tapes in her monitor you goddamn cheater!"

Anne sat up in her frame and didn't say anything. She looked confused. "You're a bunch of cheaters!" Gloria kept saying. Kromer got her by the wrists and said. "Take it easy, take it easy. You're going scape-crazy, girl."

"Don't tell me I'm crazy!" said Gloria. She twisted away from Kromer and ran to the seats. Mr. Warren was there, watching her with his hat in his hands. I ran after Gloria and said her name but she said "Leave me alone!" and went over to Mr. Warren. "You saw it, didn't you?" she said.

"I'm sorry?" said Mr. Warren.

"You must have seen it, the way she wasn't moving at all," said Gloria. "Come on, tell these cheaters you saw it. I'll go on that date with you if you tell them."

"I'm sorry, darling. I was looking at you."

Kromer knocked me out of the way and grabbed Gloria from behind. "Listen to me, girl. You're hallucinating. You're scape-happy. We see it all the time." He was talking quiet but hard. "Any more of this and you're out of the

143

show, you understand? Get in the back and lie down now and get some sleep. You need it."

"You bastard," said Gloria.

"Sure, I'm a bastard, but you're seeing things." He held Gloria's wrist and she sagged.

Mr. Warren got up and put his hat on. "I'll see you tomorrow, darling. Don't worry. I'm rooting for you." He went out.

Gloria didn't look at him.

Kromer took Gloria back to the rest area but suddenly I wasn't paying much attention myself. I had been thinking Fearing wasn't taking advantage of the free action by talking about it because there wasn't anyone much in the place to impress at this hour. Then I looked around and I realized there were two people missing and that was Fearing and Lane.

I found Ed and I asked him if Lane had dropped out of the contest and he said no.

"Maybe there's a way you could find out if Anne is really scaping or if she's a cheat," I said to Mr. Sneeze.

"I don't see how I could," he said. "I can't visit her, she has to visit me. And nobody visits me except you." He hopped and jiggled in his five places. "I'd like it if I could meet Gloria and Lane."

"Let's not talk about Lane," I said.

When I saw Fearing again I couldn't look at him. He was out talking to the people who came by in the morning, not in the microphone but one at a time, shaking hands and taking compliments like it was him doing the scaping.

There were only eight people left in the contest. Lane was still in it but I didn't care.

I knew if I tried to sleep I would just lie there thinking. So I went to rinse out under my suit, which was getting pretty rank. I hadn't been out of that suit since the contest started. In the bathroom I looked out the little window at the daylight and I thought about how I hadn't been out of that building for five days either, no matter how much I'd gone to Mars and elsewhere.

I went back in and saw Gloria asleep and I thought all of a sudden that I should try to win.

But maybe that was just the idea coming over me that Gloria wasn't going to.

I didn't notice it right away because I went to other places first. Mr. Sneeze had made me promise I'd always have something new to tell him about so I always opened a few drawers. I went to a tank game but it was boring. Then I found a place called the American History Blood And Wax Museum and I stopped President Lincoln from getting murdered a couple of times. I tried to stop President Kennedy from getting murdered but if I stopped it one way it always happened a different way. I don't know why.

So then I was going to tell Mr. Sneeze about it and that's when I found out. I went into his drawer and touched the right numbers but what I got wasn't the usual five pictures of the snowman. It was pieces of him but chopped up and stretched into thin white strips, around the edge of the black space, like a band of white light.

I said, "Mr. Sneeze?"

There wasn't any voice.

I went out and came back in but it was the same. He couldn't talk. The band of white strips got narrower and wider, like it was trying to move or talk. It looked a bit like a hand waving open and shut. But if he was still there he couldn't talk.

I would have taken my mask off then anyway, but the heat of my face and my tears forced me to.

I saw Fearing up front talking and I started for him without even getting my suit unclipped, so I tore up a few of my wires. I didn't care. I knew I was out now. I went right out and tackled Fearing from behind. He wasn't so big, anyway. Only his voice was big. I got him down on the floor.

"You killed him," I said, and I punched him as hard as I could, but you know Kromer and Gilmartin were there holding my arms before I could hit him more than once. I just screamed at Fearing, "You killed him, you killed him."

Fearing was smiling at me and wiping his mouth. "Your snowman malfunctioned, kid."

"That's a lie!"

"You were boring us to death with that snowman, you little punk. Give it a rest, for chrissake."

I kept kicking out even though they had me pulled away from him. "I'll kill you!" I said.

"Right," said Fearing. "Throw him out of here."

He never stopped smiling. Everything suited his plans, that was what I hated.

Kromer the big ape and Gilmartin pulled me outside into the sunlight and it was like a knife in my eyes. I couldn't believe how bright it was. They tossed me down in the street and when I got up Kromer punched me, hard.

Then Gloria came outside. I don't know how she found out, if she heard me screaming or if Ed woke her. Anyway she gave Kromer a pretty good punch in the side and said "Leave him alone!"

Kromer was surprised and he moaned and I got away

from him. Gloria punched him again. Then she turned around and gave Gilmartin a kick in the nuts and he went down. I'll always remember in spite of what happened next that she gave those guys a couple they'd be feeling for a day or two.

The gang who beat the crap out of us were a mix of the militia and some other guys from the town, including Lane's boyfriend. Pretty funny that he'd take out his frustration on us, but that just shows you how good Fearing had that whole town wrapped around his finger.

Outside of town we found an old house that we could hide in and get some sleep. I slept longer than Gloria. When I woke up she was on the front steps rubbing a spoon back and forth on the pavement to make a sharp point, even though I could see it hurt her arm to do it.

"Well, we did get fed for a couple of days," I said.

Gloria didn't say anything.

"Let's go up to San Francisco," I said. "There's a lot of lonely women there."

I was making a joke of course.

Gloria looked at me. "What's that supposed to mean?"

"Just that maybe I can get us in for once."

Gloria didn't laugh, but I knew she would later.

Five Fucks

1

"I feel different from other people. Really different. Yet whenever I have a conversation with a new person it turns into a discussion of things we have in common. Work, places, feelings. Whatever. It's the way people talk, I know, I share the blame, I do it too. But I want to stop and shout no, it's not like that, it's not the same for me. I feel different."

"I understand what you mean."

"That's not the right response."

"I mean what the fuck are you talking about."

"Right." Laughter.

She lit a cigarette while E. went on.

"The notion is like a linguistic virus. It makes any conversation go all pallid and reassuring. 'Oh, I know, it's like that for me too.' But the virus isn't content just to eat conversations, it wants to destroy lives. It wants you to fall in love."

"There are worse things."

"Not for me."

"Famine, war, floods."

"Those never happened to me. Love did. Love is the worst thing that ever happened to me."

"That's fatuous."

"What's the worst thing that ever happened to you?"

She was silent for a full minute.

"But there, *that's* the first fatuous thing I've said. Asking you to consider *my* situation by consulting *your* experience. You see? The virus is loose again. I don't want you to agree that our lives are the same. They aren't. I just want you to listen to what I say seriously, to believe me."

"I believe you."

"Don't say it in that tone of voice. All breathy."

"Fuck you." She laughed again.

"Do you want another drink?"

"In a minute." She slurped at what was left in her glass, then said, "You know what's funny?"

"What?"

"Other people do feel the way you do, that they're apart from everyone else. It's the same as the way every time you fall in love it feels like something new, even though you do the exact same things over again. Feeling unique is what we all have in common, it's the thing that's always the same."

"No, I'm different. And falling in love is different for me each time, different things happen. Bad things."

"But you're still the same as you were before the first time. You just feel different."

"No, I've changed. I'm much worse."

"You're not bad."

"You should have seen me before. Do you want another drink?"

The laminated place mat on the table between them showed pictures of exotic drinks. "This one," she said. "A zombie." It was purple.

"You don't want that."

"Yes I do. I love zombies."

"No you don't. You've never had one. Anyway, this place makes a terrible zombie." He ordered two more margaritas.

"You're such an expert."

"Only on zombies."

"On zombies and love is bad."

"You're making fun of me. I thought you promised to take me seriously, believe me."

"I was lying. People always lie when they flirt."

"We're not flirting."

"Then what are we doing?"

"We're just drinking, drinking and talking. And I'm trying to warn you."

"And you're staring."

"You're beautiful. Oh God."

"That reminds me of one. What's the worst thing about being an atheist?"

"I give up."

"No one to talk to when you come."

2

Morning light seeped through the macrame curtain and freckled the rug. Motes seemed to boil from its surface. For a moment she thought the rug was somehow on the ceiling, then his cat ran across it, yowling at her. The cat looked starved. She was lying on her stomach in his loft bed, head over the side. He was gone. She lay tangled in the humid sheets, feeling her own body.

Lover—she thought.

She could barely remember.

She found her clothes, then went and rinsed her face in the kitchen sink. A film of shaved hairs lined the porcelain bowl. She swirled it out with hot water, watched as the slow drain gulped it away. The drain sighed.

The table was covered with unopened mail. On the back of an envelope was a note: *I don't want to see you again. Sorry. The door locks.* She read it twice, considering each word, working it out like another language. The cat crept into the kitchen. She dropped the envelope.

She put her hand down and the cat rubbed against it. Why was it so thin? It didn't look old. The fact of the note was still sinking in. She remembered the night only in flashes, visceral strobe. With her fingers she combed the tangles out of her hair. She stood up and the cat dashed away. She went out into the hall, undecided, but the weighted door latched behind her.

Fuck him.

The problem was of course that she wanted to.

It was raining. She treated herself to a cab on Eighth Avenue. In the backseat she closed her eyes. The potholes felt like mines, and the cab squeaked like rusty bedsprings. It was Sunday. Coffee, corn muffin, newspaper; she'd insulate herself with them, make a buffer between the night and the new day.

But there was something wrong with the doorman at her building.

"You're back!" he said.

She was led incredulous to her apartment full of dead houseplants and unopened mail, her answering machine full of calls from friends, clients, the police. There was a layer of dust on the answering machine. Her address book and laptop disks were gone; clues, the doorman explained.

"Clues to what?"

"Clues to your case. To what happened to you. Everyone was worried."

"Well, there's nothing to worry about. I'm fine."

"Everyone had theories. The whole building."

"I understand."

151

"The man in charge is a good man, Miss Rush. The building feels a great confidence in him."

"Good."

"I'm supposed to call him if something happens, like someone trying to get into your place, or you coming back. Do you want me to call?"

"Let me call."

The card he handed her was bent and worn from traveling in his pocket. CORNELL PUPKISS, MISSING PERSONS. And a phone number. She reached out her hand; there was dust on the telephone too. "Please go," she said.

"Is there anything you need?"

"No." She thought of E.'s cat, for some reason.

"You can't tell me at least what happened?"

"No."

She remembered E.'s hands and mouth on her—a week ago? An hour?

Cornell Pupkiss was tall and drab and stolid, like a man built on the model of a tower of suitcases. He wore a hat and a trench coat, and shoes which were filigreed with a thousand tiny scratches, as though they'd been beset by phonograph needles. He seemed to absorb and deaden light.

On the telephone he had insisted on seeing her. He'd handed her the disks and the address book at the door. Now he stood just inside the door and smiled gently at her.

"I wanted to see you in the flesh," he said. "I've come to know you from photographs and people's descriptions. When I come to know a person in that manner I like to see them in the flesh if I can. It makes me feel I've completed my job, a rare enough illusion in my line."

There was nothing bright or animated in the way he

spoke. His voice was like furniture with the varnish carefully sanded off. "But I haven't really completed my job until I understand what happened," he went on. "Whether a crime was committed. Whether you're in some sort of trouble with which I can help."

She shook her head.

"Where were you?" he said.

"I was with a man."

"I see. For almost two weeks?"

"Yes."

She was still holding the address book. He raised his large hand in its direction, without uncurling a finger to point. "We called every man you know."

"This—this was someone I just met. Are these questions necessary, Mr. Pupkiss?"

"If the time was spent voluntarily, no." His lips tensed, his whole expression deepened, like gravy jelling. "I'm sorry, Miss Rush."

Pupkiss in his solidity touched her somehow. Reassured her. If he went away, she saw now, she'd be alone with the questions. She wanted him to stay a little longer and voice the questions for her.

But now he was gently sarcastic. "You're answerable to no one, of course. I only suggest that in the future you might spare the concern of your neighbors, and the effort of my department—a single phone call would be sufficient."

"I didn't realize how much time had passed," she said. He couldn't know how truthful that was.

"I've heard it can be like that," he said, surprisingly bitter. "But it's not criminal to neglect the feelings of others; just adolescent."

You don't understand, she nearly cried out. But she saw that he would view it as one or the other, a menace or

153

self-indulgence. If she convinced him of her distress, he'd want to protect her.

She couldn't let harm come to E. She wanted to comprehend what had happened, but Pupkiss was too blunt to be her investigatory tool.

Reflecting in this way, she said, "The things that happen to people don't always fit into such easy categories as that."

"I agree," he said, surprising her again. "But in my job it's best to keep from bogging down in ontology. Missing Persons is an extremely large and various category. Many people are lost in relatively simple ways, and those are generally the ones I can help. Good day, Miss Rush."

"Good day." She didn't object as he moved to the door. Suddenly she was eager to be free of this ponderous man, his leaden integrity. She wanted to be left alone to remember the night before, to think of the one who'd devoured her and left her reeling. That was what mattered.

E. had somehow caused two weeks to pass in one feverish night, but Pupkiss threatened to make the following morning feel like two weeks.

He shut the door behind him so carefully that there was only a little huff of displaced air and a tiny click as the bolt engaged.

"It's me," she said into the intercom.

There was only static. She pressed the button again. "Let me come up."

He didn't answer, but the buzzer at the door sounded. She went into the hall and upstairs to his door.

"It's open," he said.

E. was seated at the table, holding a drink. The cat was curled up on the pile of envelopes. The apartment was dark. Still, she saw what she hadn't before: he lived terribly, in rooms that were wrecked and provisional. The plaster was cracked everywhere. Cigarette stubs were bunched in the baseboard corners where, having still smoldered, they'd tanned the linoleum. The place smelled sour, in a way that made her think of the sourness she'd washed from her body in her own bath an hour before.

He tilted his head up, but didn't meet her gaze. "Why are you here?"

"I wanted to see you."

"You shouldn't."

His voice was ragged, his expression had a crushed quality. His hand on the glass was tensed like a claw. But even diminished and bitter he seemed to her effervescent, made of light.

"We—something happened when we made love," she said. The words came tenderly. "We lost time."

"I warned you. Now leave."

"My life," she said, uncertain what she meant.

"Yes, it's yours," he shot back. "Take it and go."

"If I gave you two weeks, it seems the least you can do is look me in the eye," she said.

He did it, but his mouth trembled as though he were guilty or afraid. His face was beautiful to her.

"I want to know you," she said.

"I can't let that happen," he said. "You see why." He tipped his glass back and emptied it, grimacing.

"This is what always happens to you?"

"I can't answer your questions."

"If that happens, I don't care." She moved to him and put her hands in his hair.

He reached up and held them there.

3

A woman has come into my life. I hardly know how to speak of it.

I was in the station, enduring the hectoring of Dell Armickle, the commander of the Vice Squad. He is insufferable, a toad from Hell. He follows the donut cart through the offices each afternoon, pinching the buttocks of the Jamaican woman who peddles the donuts and that concentrated urine others call coffee. This day he stopped at my desk to gibe at the headlines in my morning paper. "Union Boss Stung In Fat Farm Sex Ring—ha! Made you look, didn't I?"

"What?"

"Pupkiss, you're only pretending to be thick. How much you got hidden away in that Swedish bank account by now?"

"Sorry?" His gambits were incomprehensible.

"Whatsis?" he said, poking at my donut, ignoring his own blather better than I could ever hope to. "Cinnamon?"

"Whole wheat," I said.

Then she appeared. She somehow floated in without causing any fuss, and stood at the head of my desk. She was pale and hollow-eyed and beautiful, like Renée Falconetti in Dreyer's *Jeanne d'Arc*.

"Officer Pupkiss," she said. Is it only in the light of what followed that I recall her speaking my name as though she knew me? At least she spoke it with certainty, not questioning whether she'd found her goal.

I'd never seen her before, though I can only prove it by tautology: I knew at that moment I was seeing a face I would never forget.

Armickle bugged his eyes and nostrils at me, imitating both clown and beast. "Speak to the lady, Cornell," he said, managing to impart to the syllables of my given name a childish ribaldry.

"I'm Pupkiss," I said awkwardly.

"I'd like to talk to you," she said. She looked only at me, as though Armickle didn't exist.

"I can take a hint," said Armickle. "Have fun, you two." He hurried after the donut cart.

"You work in Missing Persons," she said.

"No," I said. "Petty Violations."

"Before, you used to work in Missing Persons—"

"Never. They're a floor above us. I'll walk you to the elevator if you'd like."

"No." She shook her head curtly, impatiently. "Forget it. I want to talk to you. What are Petty Violations?"

"It's an umbrella term. But I'd sooner address your concerns than try your patience with my job description."

"Yes. Could we go somewhere?"

I led her to a booth in the coffee shop downstairs. I ordered a donut, to replace the one I'd left behind on my desk. She drank coffee, holding the cup with both hands to warm them. I found myself wanting to feed her, build her a nest.

"Cops really do like donuts," she said, smiling weakly.

"Or toruses," I said.

"Sorry? You mean the astrological symbol?"

"No, the geometric shape. A torus. A donut is in the shape of one. Like a life preserver, or a tire, or certain space stations. It's a little joke of mine: cops don't like donuts, they like toruses."

She looked at me oddly. I cursed myself for bringing it up. "Shouldn't the plural be *tori?*" she said.

I winced. "I'm sure you're right. Never mind. I don't mean to take up your time with my little japes."

"I've got plenty of time," she said, poignant again.

"Nevertheless. You wished to speak to me."

"You knew me once," she said.

I did my best to appear sympathetic, but I was baffled.

"Something happened to the world. Everything changed. Everyone that I know has disappeared."

"As an evocation of subjective truth—" I began.

"No. I'm talking about something real. I used to have friends."

"I've had few, myself."

"Listen to me. All the people I know have disappeared. My family, my friends, everyone I used to work with. They've all been replaced by strangers who don't know me. I have nowhere to go. I've been awake for two days looking for my life. I'm exhausted. You're the only person that looks the same as before, and has the same name. The Missing Persons man, ironically."

"I'm not the Missing Persons man," I said.

"Cornell Pupkiss. I could never forget a name like that."

"It's been a burden."

"You don't remember coming to my apartment? You said you'd been looking for me. I was gone for two weeks."

I struggled against temptation. I could extend my time in her company by playing along, indulging the misunderstanding. In other words, by betraying what I knew to be the truth: that I had nothing at all to do with her unusual situation.

"No," I said. "I don't remember."

Her expression hardened. "Why should you?" she said bitterly.

"Your question's rhetorical," I said. "Permit me a rhetorical reply. That I don't know you from some earlier

158

encounter we can both regret. However, I know you now. And I'd be pleased to have you consider me an ally."

"Thank you."

"How did you find me?"

"I called the station and asked if you still worked there."

"And there's no one else from your previous life?"

"No one—except him."

Ah.

"Tell me," I said.

She'd met the man she called E. in a bar, how long ago she couldn't explain. She described him as irresistible. I formed an impression of a skunk, a rat. She said he worked no deliberate charm on her, on the contrary seemed panicked when the mood between them grew intimate and full of promise. I envisioned a scoundrel with an act, a crafted diffidence that allured, a backpedaling attack.

He'd taken her home, of course.

"And?" I said.

"We fucked," she said. "It was good, I think. But I have trouble remembering."

The words stung. The one in particular. I tried not to be a child, swallowed my discomfort away. "You were drunk," I suggested.

"No. I mean, *yes*, but it was more than that. We weren't clumsy like drunks. We went into some kind of trance."

"He drugged you."

"No."

"How do you know?"

"What happened—it wasn't something he wanted."

"And what did happen?"

"Two weeks disappeared from my life overnight. When I got home I found I'd been considered missing. My friends

159

and family had been searching for me. You'd been called in."

"I thought your friends and family had vanished themselves. That no one knew you."

"No. That was the *second* time."

"Second time?"

"The second time we fucked." Then she seemed to remember something, and dug in her pocket. "Here." She handed me a scuffed business card: CORNELL PUPKISS, MISSING PERSONS.

"I can't believe you live this way. It's like a prison." She referred to the seamless rows of book spines that faced her in each of my few rooms, including the bedroom where we now stood. "Is it all criminology?"

"I'm not a policeman in some cellular sense," I said, and then realized the pun. "I mean, not intrinsically. They're novels, first editions."

"Let me guess; mysteries."

"I detest mysteries. I would never bring one into my home."

"Well, you have, in me."

I blushed, I think, from head to toe. "That's different," I stammered. "Human lives exist to be experienced, or possibly endured, but not solved. They resemble any other novel more than they do mysteries. Westerns, even. It's that lie the mystery tells that I detest."

"Your reading is an antidote to the simplifications of your profession, then."

"I suppose. Let me show you where the clean towels are kept."

I handed her fresh towels and linen, and took for myself a set of sheets to cover the living room sofa.

She saw that I was preparing the sofa and said, "The bed's big enough."

I didn't turn, but I felt the blood rush to the back of my neck as though specifically to meet her gaze. "It's four in the afternoon," I said. "I won't be going to bed for hours. Besides, I snore."

"Whatever," she said. "Looks uncomfortable, though. What's Barbara Pym? She sounds like a mystery writer, one of those stuffy English ones."

The moment passed, the blush faded from my scalp. I wondered later, though, whether this had been some crucial missed opportunity. A chance at the deeper intervention that was called for.

"Read it," I said, relieved at the change of subject. "Just be careful of the dust jacket."

"I may learn something, huh?" She took the book and climbed in between the covers.

"I hope you'll be entertained."

"And she doesn't snore, I guess. That was a joke, Mr. Pupkiss."

"So recorded. Sleep well. I have to return to the station. I'll lock the door."

"Back to Little Offenses?"

"Petty Violations."

"Oh, right." I could hear her voice fading. As I stood and watched, she fell soundly asleep. I took the Pym from her hands and replaced it on the shelf.

I wasn't going to the station. Using the information she'd given me, I went to find the tavern E. supposedly frequented.

I found him there, asleep in a booth, head resting on his folded arms. He looked terrible, his hair a thatch, drool leaking into his sweater arm, his eyes swollen like a fevered child's, just the picture of raffish haplessness a woman would find magnetic. Unmistakably the seedy vermin I'd projected and the idol of Miss Rush's nightmare.

I went to the bar and ordered an Irish coffee, and considered. Briefly indulging a fantasy of personal power, I rebuked myself for coming here and making him real, when he had only before been an absurd story, a neurotic symptom. Then I took out the card she'd given me and laid it on the bar top. Cornell Pupkiss, Missing Persons. No, I myself was the symptom. It is seldom as easy in practice as in principle to acknowledge one's own bystander status in incomprehensible matters.

I took my coffee to his booth and sat across from him. He roused and looked up at me.

"Rise and shine, buddy boy," I said, a little stiffly. I've never thrilled to the role of Bad Cop.

"What's the matter?"

"Your unshaven chin is scratching the table surface."

"Sorry." He rubbed his eyes.

"Got nowhere to go?"

"What are you, the house dick?"

"I'm in the employ of any taxpayer," I said. "The bartender happens to be one."

"He's never complained to me."

"Things change."

"You can say that again."

We stared at each other. I supposed he was nearly my age, though he was more boyishly pretty than I'd been even as an actual boy. I hated him for that, but I pitied him for the part I saw that was precociously old and bitter.

I thought of Miss Rush asleep in my bed. She'd been worn

and disarrayed by their two encounters, but she didn't yet look this way. I wanted to keep her from it.

"Let me give you some advice," I said, as gruffly as I could manage. "Solve your problems."

"I hadn't thought of that."

"Don't get stuck in a rut." I was aware of the lameness of my words only as they emerged, too late to stop.

"Don't worry, I never do."

"Very well then," I said, somehow unnerved. "This interview is concluded." If he'd shown any sign of budging I might have leaned back in the booth, crossed my arms authoritatively, and stared him out the door. Since he remained planted in his seat, I stood up, feeling that my last spoken words needed reinforcement.

He laid his head back into the cradle of his arms, first sliding the laminated place mat underneath. "This will protect the table surface," he said.

"That's good, practical thinking," I heard myself say as I left the booth.

It wasn't the confrontation I'd been seeking.

On the way home I shopped for breakfast, bought orange juice, milk, bagels, fresh coffee beans. I took it upstairs and unpacked it as quietly as I could in the kitchen, then removed my shoes and crept in to have a look at Miss Rush. She was peaceably asleep. I closed the door and prepared my bed on the sofa. I read a few pages of the Penguin softcover edition of Muriel Spark's *The Bachelors* before dropping off.

Before dawn, the sky like blued steel, the city silent, I was woken by a sound in the apartment, at the front door. I put on my robe and went into the kitchen. The front door was unlocked, my key in the deadbolt. I went back through the apartment; Miss Rush was gone.

I write this at dawn. I am very frightened.

163

4

In an alley which ran behind a lively commercial street there sat a pair of the large trash receptacles commonly known as Dumpsters. In them accumulated the waste produced by the shops whose rear entrances shared the alley; a framer's, a soup kitchen, an antique clothing store, a donut bakery, and a photocopyist's establishment, and by the offices above those storefronts. On this street and in this alley, each day had its seasons: Spring, when complaining morning shifts opened the shops, students and workers rushed to destinations, coffee sloshing in paper cups, and in the alley, the sanitation contractors emptied containers, sorted recyclables and waste like bees pollinating garbage truck flowers; Summer, the ripened afternoons, when the workday slackened, shoppers stole long lunches from their employers, the cafes filled with students with highlighter pens, and the indigent beckoned for the change that jingled in incautious pockets, while in the alley new riches piled up; Autumn, the cooling evening, when half the shops closed, and the street was given over to prowlers and pacers, those who lingered in bookstores and dined alone in Chinese restaurants, and the indigent plundered the fatted Dumpsters for half-eaten paper bag lunches, batches of botched donuts, wearable cardboard matting and unmatched socks, and burnable wood scraps; Winter, the selfish night, when even the cafes battened down iron gates through which nightwatchmen fluorescents palely flickered, the indigent built their overnight camps in doorways and under sidestreet hedges, or in wrecked cars, and the street itself was an abandoned stage.

On the morning in question the sun shone brightly, yet the air was bitingly cold. Birds twittered resentfully.

When the sanitation crew arrived to wheel the two Dumpsters out to be hydraulically lifted into their screeching, whining truck, they were met with cries of protest from within.

The men lifted the metal tops of the Dumpsters and discovered that an indigent person had lodged in each of them, a lady in one, a gentleman in the other.

"Geddoudadare," snarled the eldest sanitation engineer, a man with features like a spilled plate of stew.

The indigent lady rose from within the heap of refuse and stood blinking in the bright morning sun. She was an astonishing sight, a ruin. The colors of her skin and hair and clothes had all surrendered to gray; an archaeologist might have ventured an opinion as to their previous hue. She could have been anywhere between thirty and fifty years old, but speculation was absurd; her age had been taken from her and replaced with a timeless condition, a state. Her eyes were pitiable; horrified and horrifying; witnesses, victims, accusers.

"Where am I?" she said softly.

"Isedgeddoudadare," barked the garbage operative.

The indigent gentleman then raised himself from the other Dumpster. He was in every sense her match; to describe him would be to tax the reader's patience for things worn, drab, desolate, crestfallen, unfortunate, etc. He turned his head at the trashman's exhortation and saw his mate.

"What's the—" he began, then stopped.

"You," said the indigent lady, lifting an accusing finger at him from amidst her rags. "You did this to me."

"No," he said. "No."

"Yes!" she screamed.

"C'mon," said the burly sanitateur. He and his second

began pushing the nearer container, which bore the lady, towards his truck.

She cursed at them and climbed out, with some difficulty. They only laughed at her and pushed the cart out to the street. The indigent man scrambled out of his Dumpster and brushed at his clothes, as though they could thereby be distinguished from the material in which he'd lain.

The lady flew at him, furious. "Look at us! Look what you did to me!" She whirled her limbs at him, trailing banners of rag.

He backed from her, and bumped into one of the garbagemen, who said, "Hey!"

"It's not my fault," said the indigent man.

"Yugoddagedoudahere!" said the stew-faced worker.

"What do you mean it's not your fault?" she shrieked.

Windows were sliding open in the offices above them. "Quiet down there," came a voice.

"It wouldn't happen without you," he said.

At that moment a policeman rounded the corner. He was a large man named Officer McPupkiss who even in the morning sun conveyed an aspect of night. His policeman's uniform was impeccably fitted, his brass polished, but his shoetops were exceptionally scuffed and dull. His presence stilled the combatants.

"What's the trouble?" he said.

They began talking all at once; the pair of indigents, the refuse handlers, and the disgruntled office worker leaning out of his window.

"Please," said McPupkiss, in a quiet voice which was nonetheless heard by all.

"He ruined my life!" said the indigent lady raggedly.

"Ah, yes. Shall we discuss it elsewhere?" He'd already grasped the situation. He held out his arms, almost as if he wanted to embrace the two tatterdemalions, and nodded at the disposal experts, who silently resumed their labors. The indigents followed McPupkiss out of the alley.

"He ruined my life," she said again when they were on the sidewalk.

"She ruined mine," answered the gentleman.

"I wish I could believe it was all so neat," said McPupkiss. "A life is simply *ruined*; credit for the destruction goes *here* or *here*. In my own experience things are more ambiguous."

"This is one of the exceptions," said the lady. "It's strange but not ambiguous. He fucked me over."

"She was warned," he said. "She made it happen."

"The two of you form a pretty picture," said McPupkiss. "You ought to be working together to improve your situation; instead you're obsessed with blame."

"We can't work together," she said. "Anytime we come together we create a disaster."

"Fine, go your separate ways," said the officer. "I've always thought 'We got ourselves into this mess and we can get ourselves out of it' was a laughable attitude. Many things are irreversible, and what matters is moving on. For example, a car can't reverse its progress over a cliff; it has to be abandoned by those who survive the fall, if any do."

But by the end of this speech the gray figures had fallen to blows and were no longer listening. They clutched one another like exhausted boxers, hissing and slapping, each trying to topple the other. McPupkiss chided himself for wasting his breath, grabbed them both by the back of their scruffy collars, and began smiting their hindquarters with his dingy shoes until they ran down the block and out of sight together, united again, McPupkiss thought, as they were so clearly meant to be.

5

The village of Pupkinstein was nestled in a valley surrounded by steep woods. The villagers were a contented
people except for the fear of the two monsters that lived in
the woods and came into the village to fight their battles.
Everyone knew that the village had been rebuilt many times
after being half destroyed by the fighting of the monsters.
No one living could remember the last of these battles, but
that only intensified the suspicion that the next time would
surely be soon.

Finally the citizens of Pupkinstein gathered in the town
square to discuss the threat of the two monsters, and debate
proposals for the prevention of their battles. A group of
builders said, "Let us build a wall around the perimeter of
the village, with a single gate which could be fortified by
volunteer soldiers."

A group of priests began laughing, and one of them said,
"Don't you know that the monsters have wings? They'll flap
twice and be over your wall in no time."

Since none of the builders had ever seen the monsters,
they had no reply.

Then the priests spoke up and said, "We should set up
temples which can be filled with offerings: food, wine, burning candles, knitted scarves, and the like. The monsters will
be appeased."

Now the builders laughed, saying, "These are monsters,
not jealous gods. They don't care for our appeasements.
They only want to crush each other, and we're in the way."

The priests had no answer, since their holy scriptures
contained no accounts of the monsters' habits.

Then the Mayor of Pupkinstein, a large, somber man,
said, "We should build our own monster here in the middle

of the square, a scarecrow so huge and threatening that the monsters will see it and at once be frightened back into hiding."

This plan satisfied the builders, with their love of construction, and the priests, with their fondness for symbols. So the very next morning the citizens of Pupkinstein set about constructing a gigantic figure in the square. They began by demolishing their fountain. In its place they marked out the soles of two gigantic shoes, and the builders sank foundations for the towering legs that would extend from them. Then the carpenters built frames, and the seamstresses sewed canvases, and in less than a week the two shoes were complete, and the beginnings of ankles besides. Without being aware of it, the citizens had begun to model their monster on the Mayor, who was always present as a model, whereas no one had ever seen the two monsters.

The following night it rained. Tarpaulins were thrown over the half-constructed ankles that rose from the shoes. The Mayor and the villagers retired to an alehouse to toast their labors and be sheltered from the rain. But just as the proprietor was pouring their ale, someone said, "Listen!"

Between the crash of thunder and the crackle of lightning there came a hideous bellowing from the woods at either end of the valley.

"They're coming!" the citizens said. "Too soon—our monster's not finished!"

"How bitter," said one man. "We've had a generation of peace in which to build, and yet we only started a few days ago."

"We'll always know that we tried," said the Mayor philosophically.

"Perhaps the shoes will be enough to frighten them," said the proprietor, who had always been regarded as a fool.

No one answered him. Fearing for their lives, the villagers ran to their homes and barricaded themselves behind shutters and doors, hid their children in attics and potato cellars, and snuffed out candles and lanterns that might lead an attacker to their doors. No one dared even look at the naked, miserable things that came out of the woods and into the square; no one, that is, except the Mayor. He stood in the shadow of one of the enormous shoes, rain beating on his umbrella, only dimly sensing that he was watching another world being fucked away.

6

I live in a shadowless pale blue sea.

I am a bright pink crablike thing, some child artist's idea of an invertebrate, so badly drawn as to be laughable.

Nevertheless, I have feelings.

More than feelings. I have a mission, an obsession.

I am building a wall.

Every day I move a grain of sand. The watercolor sea washes over my back, but I protect my accumulation. I fasten each grain to the wall with my comic-book feces. (Stink lines hover above my shit, also flies which look like bow ties, though I am supposed to be underwater.)

He is on the other side. My nemesis. Someday my wall will divide the ocean, someday it will reach the surface, or the top of the page, and be called a reef. He will be on the other side. He will not be able to get to me.

My ridiculous body moves only sideways, but it is enough.

I will divide the watercolor ocean, I will make it two. We must have a world for each of us.

I move a grain. When I come to my wall, paradoxically, I

am nearest him. His little pink body, practically glowing. He is watching me, watching me build.

There was a time when he tried to help, when every day for a week he added a grain to my wall. I spent every day that week removing his grain, expelling it from the wall, and no progress was made until he stopped. He understands now. My wall must be my own. We can be together in nothing. Let him build his own wall. So he watches.

My wall will take me ten thousand years to complete. I live only for the day that it is complete.

The Pupfish floats by.

The Pupfish is a fish with the features of a mournful hound dog and a policeman's cap. The Pupfish is the only creature in the sea apart from me and my pink enemy.

The Pupfish, I know, would like to scoop me up in its oversized jaws and take me away. The Pupfish thinks it can solve my problem.

But no matter how far the Pupfish took me, I would still be in the same ocean with *him*. That cannot be. There must be two oceans. So I am building a wall.

I move a grain.

I rest.

I will be free.

The Hardened Criminals

The day we went to paint our names on the prison built of hardened criminals was the first time I had ever been there. I'd seen pictures, mostly video footage shot from a helicopter. The huge building was still as a mountain, but the camera was always in motion, as though a single angle was insufficient to convey the truth about the prison.

The overhead footage created two contradictory impressions. The prison was an accomplishment, a monument to human ingenuity, like a dam or an aircraft carrier. At the same time the prison was a disaster, something imposed by nature on the helpless city, a pit gouged by a meteorite, or a forest-fire scar.

Footage from inside the prison, of the wall, was rare.

Carl Hemphill was my best friend in junior high school. In three years we had graduated together from video games to petty thievery, graffiti, and pot smoking. It was summer now, and we were headed for two different high schools. Knowledge that we would be drawn into separate worlds lurked indefinably in our silences.

Carl involved me in the expedition to the prison wall. He was the gadfly, moving easily between the rebel cliques that rarely attended class—spending the school day in the park outside, instead—and those still timid and obedient, like myself. Our group that day included four other boys, two of them older, dropouts from our junior high who were passing their high school years in the park. For them, I imagined, this was a visit to one of their own possible futures: they might be inside someday. For me it was not that but something else, a glimpse of a repressed past. My father was a part of the prison.

It was a secret not only from the rest of our impromptu party, but from Carl, from the entire school. If asked, I said my father had died when I was six, and that I couldn't remember him, didn't know him except in snapshots, anecdotes. The last part of the lie was true. I knew of my father, but I couldn't remember him.

To reach the devastated section that had been the center of the city we first had to cross or skirt the vast Chinese ghetto, whose edge was normally an absolute limit to our wanderings. In fact, there was a short buffer zone where on warehouse doors our graffiti overlapped with the calligraphs painted by the Chinese gangs. Courage was measured by how deep into this zone your tag still appeared, how often it obliterated the Chinese writing. Carl and one of the older boys were already rattling their spray cans. We would extend our courage today.

The trip was uneventful at first. Our nervous pack moved down side streets and alleys, through the mists of steaming sewers, favoring the commercial zone where we could retreat into some Chinese merchant's shop and not be isolated in a lot or alley. The older Chinese ignored us, or at most shook their heads. We might as well have been stray dogs. When we came to a block of warehouses or boarded shops, we found a suitable door or wall and tagged up, reproducing with spray paint those signature icons we'd laboriously perfected with ballpoint on textbook covers and desktops. Only two or three of us would tag up at a given stop before we panicked and hurried away, spray cans thrust back under our coats. We were hushed, respectful, even as we defaced the territory.

We were at a freeway overpass, through the gang zone, we thought, when they found us. Nine Chinese boys, every one of them verging on manhood the way only two in our party were. Had they been roaming in such a large pack and found us by luck, or had one or another of them (or even an older Chinese, a shopkeeper perhaps) sighted us earlier and sounded a call-to-arms? We couldn't know. They closed around us like a noose in the shadow of the overpass, and instantly there was no question of fighting or running. We would wait, petrified. They would deliver a verdict.

It was Carl who stepped forward and told them that we were going to the prison. One of them pushed him back into our group, but the information triggered a fastpaced squabble in Chinese. We listened hard, though we couldn't understand a word.

Finally a question was posed, in English. "Why you going there?"

The oldest in our group, a dropout named Richard, surprised us by answering. "My brother's inside," he said. None of us had known.

He'd volunteered his secret in the cause of obtaining our passage. I should have chimed in now with mine. But my father wasn't a living prisoner inside, he was a part of the wall. I didn't speak.

The Chinese gang began moving us along the empty street, nudging us forward with small pushes and scoffing commands. Soon enough, though, these spurs fell away. The older boys became our silent escort, our bodyguards. In that manner we moved out of the ghetto, the zone of warehouses and cobblestone, to the edge of the old downtown.

174

The office blocks here had been home to squatters before being completely abandoned, and many windows still showed some temporary decoration: ragged curtains, cardboard shutters, an arrangement of broken dolls or toys on the sill. Other windows were knocked out, the frames tarnished by fire.

The Chinese boys slackened around us as the prison tower came into view. One of them pointed at it, and pushed Carl, as though to say, *If that's what you came for, go.* We hurried up, out of the noose of the gang, towards the prison. None of us dared look back to question the gift of our release. Anyway, we were hypnotized by the tower.

The surrounding buildings had been razed so that the prison stood alone on a blasted heath of concrete and earth five blocks wide, scattered with broken glass and twisted tendrils of orange steel. Venturing into this huge clearing out of the narrow streets seemed dangerously stupid, as though we were prey coming from the forest to drink at an exposed water hole. We might not have done it without the gang somewhere at our back. As it was, our steps faltered.

The tower was only ten or eleven stories tall then, but in that cleared space it already seemed tremendous. It stood unfenced, nearly a block wide, and consummately dark and malignant, the uneven surfaces absorbing the glaring winter light. We moved towards it across the concrete. I understand now that it was intended that we be able to approach it, that striking fear in young hearts was the point of the tower, but at the time I marveled that there was nothing between us and the wall of criminals, that no guards or dogs or klaxons screamed a warning to move away.

They'd been broken before being hardened. That was the first shock. I'd envisioned some clever fit, a weaving of limbs, as in an Escher print. It wasn't quite that pretty. Their legs and shoulders had been crushed into the corners of a block, like compacted garbage, and the fit was the simple, inhuman one of right angle flush against right angle. The wall bulged with crumpled limbs, squeezed so tightly together that they resembled a frieze carved in stone, and it was impossible to picture them unfolded, restored. Their heads were tucked inside the prison, so the outer wall was made of backs, folded swollen legs, feet back against buttocks, and squared shoulders.

My father had been sentenced to the wall when it was already at least eight stories high, I knew. He wasn't down here, this couldn't be him we defaced. I didn't have to think of him, I told myself. This visit had nothing to do with him.

Almost as one, and still in perfect silence, we reached out to touch the prison. It was as hard as rock but slightly warm. Scars, imperfections in the skin, all had been sealed into an impenetrable surface. We knew the bricks couldn't feel anything, yet it seemed obscene to touch them, to do more than poke once or twice to satisfy our curiosity.

Finally, we required some embarrassment to break the silence. One of the older boys said, "Get your hand off his butt, you faggot."

We laughed, and jostled one another, as the Chinese gang had jostled us, to show that we didn't care. Then the boys with spray cans drew them out.

The prison wall was already thick with graffiti from the ground to a spot perhaps six feet up, where it trailed off. There were just a few patches of flesh or tattoo visible between the trails of paint. A few uncanny tags floated above reach, where the canvas of petrified flesh was clearer. I suppose some ambitious taggers had stood on one another's shoulders, or dragged some kind of makeshift ladder across the waste.

We weren't going to manage anything like that. But our paint would be the newest, the outermost layer, at least for a while. One by one we tagged up, offering the wall the largest and most elaborated versions of our glyphs. After my turn I stepped up close to watch the paint set, the juicy electric gleam slowly fading to matte on the minutely knobby surface of hardened flesh.

Then I stepped back. From a distance of ten feet our work was already nearly invisible. I squinted into the bright sky and tried to count the floors, thinking of my father. At that height the bricks were indistinguishable. Not that I'd recognize the shape of my father's back or buttocks even up close, or undistorted by the compacting. I'm not even sure I'd have recognized his face.

A wind rose. We crossed the plain of concrete, hands in our pockets, into the shelter of the narrow streets, the high ruined offices. We were silent again, our newfound jauntiness expelled with the paint.

They were on us at the same overpass, the moment we came under its shadow. The deferred ambush was delivered now. They knocked us to the ground, displayed knives, took away our paint and money. They took Carl's watch. Each time we stood up they knocked us down again. When they let us go it was one at a time, sent running down the street, back into the Chinese commercial street alone, a display for the shopkeepers and deliverymen, who this time jeered and snickered.

I think we were grateful to them, ultimately. The humiliation justified our never boasting about the trip to the prison wall, our hardly speaking of it back at school or in the park. At the same time, the beating served as an easy repository for the shame we felt, a shame that would otherwise have attached to our own acts, at the wall.

In fact, we six never congregated again, as though doing so would bring the moment dangerously close. I only once ever again saw the older dropout, the one whose brother was in the prison. It was during a game of touch football in the park, and he went out of his way to bully me.

Carl and I drifted apart soon after entering separate schools. I expected to know him again later. As it happened, I missed my chance.

"Stickney," the guard called, and the man on my right stepped forward.

By the time I entered the prison, it was thirty-two stories high. I was nineteen and a fool. I'd finished high school, barely, and I was living at home, telling myself I'd apply to the state college, but not doing it. I'd been up all night drinking with the worst of the high-school crowd when I was invited along as an afterthought to what became my downfall, my chance to be a bystander at my own crime. I drove a stolen car as a getaway in a bungled armored-car robbery, and my distinction was that I drove it into the door of a black-and-white, spilling a lieutenant's morning coffee and crushing his left forearm. The trial was suffused with a vague air of embarrassment. The judge didn't mention my father.

"Martell."

I'd arrived in a group of six, driven in an otherwise empty bus through underground passages to the basement of the prison, and ushered from there to a holding area. None of us were there to be hardened and built into the prison. We were all first-time offenders, meant to live inside and be frightened, warned onto the path of goodness by the plight of the bricks.

"Pierce."

We stood together, our bodies tense with fear, our thoughts desperately narrowed. The fecal odor of the prison alone overwhelmed us. The cries that echoed down, reduced to whispers. The anticipation of the faces in the wall. We turned from each other in shame of letting it show, and we prayed as they processed us and led us away that we would be assigned different cells, different floors, and never have to see one another. Better to face the sure cruelties of the experienced convicts than have our green terror mirrored.

"Deeds, Minkowitz."

I was alone. The man at the desk flickered the papers before him, but he wasn't looking at them. When he said my name, it was a question, though by elimination he should have been certain. "Nick Marra?"

"Yes," I said.

"Put him in the hole," he said to the guards who remained.

I must have aged ten years by the time they released me from that dark nightmare, though it lasted only a week. When the door first slammed, I actually felt it as a relief: that I was hidden away and alone, after preparing or failing to prepare for cellmates, initiations, territorial conflicts. I cowered down at the middle of the floor, holding my knees to my chest, feeling myself pound like one huge heart. I tried closing my eyes but they insisted on staying open, on trying to make out a hint of form in the swirling blackness. Then I heard the voices.

"Bad son of a bitch. That's all."

"—crazy angles on it, always need to play the crazy angles, that's what Lucky says—"

"C'mere. Closer. Right here, c'mon."

"Don't let him tell you what—"

"Motherfuck."

"—live like a pig in a house you can't ever go in without wanting to kill her I didn't think like that I wasn't a killer in my own mind—"

"Wanna get laid? Wanna get some?"

"Gotta get out of here, talk to Missing Persons, *man*. They got the answers."

"Henry?"

"Don't listen to him—"

They'd fallen silent for a moment as the guards tossed me into the hole, been stunned into silence perhaps by the rare glimpse of light, but they were never silent again. That was all the bricks were, anymore, voices and ears and eyes; the chips that had been jammed into their petrified brains preserved those capacities and nothing more. So they watched and talked, and the ones in the hole just talked. I learned how to plug my ears with shreds from my clothing soon enough, but it wasn't sufficient to block out the murmur. Sleeping through the talk was the first skill to master in the prison built from criminal bricks, and I mastered it alone in the dark.

Now I went to the wall and felt the criminals. Their fronts formed a glossy, encrusted whole, hands covering genitals, knees crushed into corners that were flush against blocked shoulders. I remembered that long-ago day at the wall. Then my finger slipped into a mouth.

I yelped and pulled it out. I'd felt the teeth grind, hard, and it was only luck that I wasn't bitten. The insensate lips hadn't been aware of my finger, of course. The mouth was horribly dry and rough inside, not like living flesh, but it lived in its way, grinding out words without needing to pause for breath. I reached out again, felt the eyes. Useless here in the hole, but they blinked and rolled, as though searching, like mine. The mouth I'd touched went on, "—never want to be in Tijuana with nothing to do, be fascinating for about three days and then you'd start to go crazy—" The voice plodding, exhausted.

I'd later see how few of the hardened spoke at all, how many had retreated into themselves, eyes and mouths squeezed shut. There were dead ones, too, here and everywhere in the wall. Living prisoners had killed the most annoying bricks by carving into the stony foreheads and smashing the chips that kept the brain alive. Others had malfunctioned and died on their own. But in the dark the handful of voices seemed hundreds, more than the wall of one room could possibly hold.

"C'mere, I'm over here. Christ."

I found the one that called out.

"What you do, kid?"

"Robbery," I said.

"What you do to get thrown in *here*? Shiv a hack?"

"What?"

"You knife a guard, son?"

I didn't speak. Other voices rattled and groaned around me.

"My name's Jimmy Shand," said the confiding voice. I thought of a man who'd sit on a crate in front of a gas station. "I've been in a few knife situations, I'm not ashamed of that. Why'd you get thrown in the bucket, Peewee?"

"I didn't do anything."

"You're here."

"I didn't do anything. I just got here, on the bus. They put me in here."

"Liar."

"They checked my name and threw me in here."

"Lying motherfucker. Show some respect for your *fucking*

181

elders." He began making a sound with his mummified throat, a staccato crackling noise, as if he wanted to spit at me. I backed away to the middle of the floor, and his voice blended into the horrible, chattering mix.

I picked the corner opposite the door and away from the wall for my toilet, and slept huddled against the door. I was woken the next morning by a cold metal tray pressing against the back of my neck as it was shoved through a slot in the door. Light flashed through the gap, blindingly bright to my deprived eyes, then disappeared. The tray slid to the floor, its contents mixing. I ate the meal without knowing what it was.

"Gimme some of that, I hear you eating, you sonovabitch."

"Leave him alone, you constipated turd."

They fed me twice a day, and those incidental shards of light were my hope, my grail. I lived huddled and waiting, quietly masturbating or gnawing my cuticles, sucking precious memories dry by overuse. I quickly stopped answering the voices, and prayed that the bricks in the walls of the ordinary cells were not so malicious and insane. Of course, by the time I was sprung, I was a little insane myself.

They dragged me out through a corridor I couldn't see for the ruthless light, and into a concrete shower, where they washed me like I was a dog. Only then was I human enough to be spoken to. "Put these on, Marra." I took the clothes and dressed.

The man waiting in the office they led me to next didn't introduce himself. He didn't have the gray deadness in his features that I already associated with prison staff.

"Sit down."

I sat.

"Your father is Floyd Marra?"

182

"Why?" I meant to ask why I'd been put in isolation. My voice, stilled for days, came out a croak.

"Leave the questions to us," said the man at the desk, not unkindly. "Your father is Floyd Marra?"

"Yes."

"You need a glass of water? Get him a glass of water, Graham." One of the guards went into the next room and came back with a paper cone filled with water and handed it to me. The man at the desk pursed his lips and watched me intently as I drank.

"You're a smart guy, a high-school graduate," he said.

I nodded and put the paper cone on the desk between us. He reached over and crumpled it into a ball and tossed it under the desk.

"You're going to work for us."

"What?" I still meant to ask *why*, but he had me confused. A part of me was still in the hole. Maybe some part would be always.

"You want a cigarette?" he said. The guard called Graham was smoking. I did want one, so I nodded. "Give him a cigarette, Graham. There you go."

I smoked, and trembled, and watched the man smile.

"We're putting you in with him. You're going to be our ears, Nick. There's stuff we need to know."

I haven't seen my father since I was six years old, I wanted to say. I can't remember him. "What stuff?" I said.

"You don't need to know that now. Just get acquainted, get going on the heart-to-hearts. We'll be in touch. Graham here runs your block. He'll be your regular contact. He'll let me know when you're getting somewhere."

I looked at Graham. Just a guard, a prison heavy. Unlike the man at the desk.

"Your father's near the ceiling, lefthand, beside the upper bunk. You won't have anyone in the cell with you."

"Everybody's going to think you're hot shit, a real killer," said Graham, his first words. The other guard nodded.

"Yes, well," said the man at the desk. "So there shouldn't be any problem. And Nick?"

"Yes?" I'd already covered my new clothes with sweat, though it wasn't hot.

"Don't blow this for us. I trust you understand your options. Here, stub out the coffin nail. You're not looking so good."

I lay in the lower bunk trying not to look at the wall, trying not to make out differences in the double layer of voices, those from inside my cell, from the wall, and those of the other living prisoners that echoed in the corridor beyond. Only when the lights on the block went out did I open my eyes—I was willing myself back into the claustrophobic safety of the hole. But I couldn't sleep.

I crawled into the upper bunk.

"Floyd?" I said.

In the scant light from the corridor I could see the eyes of the wall turn to me. The bodies could have been sculpture, varnished stone, but the shifting eyes and twitching mouths were alive, more alive than I wanted them to be. The surface was layered with defacements and graffiti, not the massive spray-paint boasts of the exterior but scratched-in messages, complex engravings. And then there were the smearings, shit or food, I didn't want to know.

"—horseshoe crab, that's a hell of a thing—"

"—the hardest nut in the case—"

"—ran the table, I couldn't miss, man. Guy says John's gonna beat that nigger and I say—"

The ones that cared to have an audience piped up. There were four talkers in the upper part of the wall of my cell. I'd soon get to know them all. Billy Lancing was a black man who talked about his career as a pool hustler, lucid monologues reflecting on his own cleverness and puzzling bitterly over his downfall. Ivan Detbar, who plotted breaks and worried prison hierarchies as though he were not an immobile irrelevant presence in the wall. And John Jones—that was Billy's name for him—who was insane.

The one I noticed now was the one who said, "I'm Floyd."

A muscle in my chest punched upwards against my windpipe like a fist. I couldn't speak, couldn't think. Would meeting my father trigger the buried memories? The emotion I felt was virtual emotion. I didn't know this man. I should.

I was trembling all over.

He was missing an eye. From the crushed rim of the socket it looked like it had been pried out of the hardened flesh of the wall, not lost before. And his arms, crossed over his stomach, were scored with tiny marks, as though someone had used him to count their time in the cell. But his one eye lived, examined mine, blinked sadly. "I'm Floyd," he said again.

"My name is Nick," I said, wondering if he'd recognize it, and perhaps ask my last name. He couldn't possibly recognize me. After my week in the hole I looked as far from my six-year-old self as I ever would.

"Ever see a horseshit crap, Nick?" said John Jones.

"Shut up, Jones," said Billy Lancing.

"How'd you know my name?" said my father.

"I'm Nick Marra," I said.

"How'd you know my name?" he said again.

"You're a famous fuck," said Ivan Detbar. "Word is going

around. 'Floyd is the man around here.' All the young guys want to see if they can take you."

"Horseshoe crab, horseradish fish," said John Jones. "That's a hell of a thing. You ever see—"

"Shut up."

"You're Floyd Marra," I said.

"I'm Floyd."

I turned away, momentarily overcome. My father's plight overwhelmed mine. The starkness of this punishment suddenly was real to me, in a way it hadn't been in the hole. This view out over the bunk and through the bars, into the corridor, was the only view my father had seen since his hardening.

"I'm Nick Marra," I said. "Your son."

"I don't have a son."

I tried to establish our relationship. He agreed that he'd known a woman named Doris Thayer. That was my mother's name. His pocked mouth tightened and he said, "Tell me about Doris. Remind me of that."

I told him about Doris. He listened intently—or I thought he was listening intently. Whenever I paused, he asked a question to keep me on the subject. At the end he said only, "I remember the woman you mean." I waited, then he added, "I remember a few different women, you know. Some more trouble than they're worth. Doris I wouldn't mind seeing again."

Awkwardly, I said, "Do you remember a boy?"

"Cheesedog crab," said Jones. "That's a good one. They'll nip at you from under the surf—"

"You fucking loony."

"A boy?"

"Yes."

"Yes, there was a boy—" All at once my father began a

186

rambling whispered reminiscence, about *his* father, and about himself as a boy in the Italian ghetto. I leaned back on the bunk and looked away from the wall, towards the bars and the trickle of light from the hallway as he told me of merciless beatings, mysterious night-time uprootings from one home to another, and abandonment.

Around us the other voices from the wall babbled on, as constant as television. I was already learning to tune them out like some natural background, crickets, surf pounding. Now even my father's voice wove into the curtain around my exhausted senses. I fell asleep to the sound of his voice.

The next morning I joined the prison community. The two-tiered cafeteria called Mess Nine was a churning, teeming place, impossible not to see as a hive. Like the offices, it was on the interior, away from the living wall. I escaped notice until I took my full tray out towards the tables.

"Hey, lonely boy."

"He's not lonely, he's a psycho. Aren't you, man?"

"They're afraid of this skinny little guy, he's got to be psycho."

"Who you kill?"

I went and set my tray on an empty corner of a table and sat down, but it didn't stop. The inmate who'd latched on first ("lonely boy") followed and sat behind me.

"He needs his privacy, can't you see?" said someone else. "Let him eat and go back to his psycho cell."

"He can't socialize."

"I'll socialize him."

"He wants to fuck the wall."

"He was up late fucking the wall last night for sure. Little hung over, lonely boy?"

Fuck the wall, I came to know, was an all-purpose phrase, in constant use either as insult or as an expression of rebellion, of yearning, of ironic futility. The standing assumption was that the dry, corroded mouths would gnaw a man's penis to bloody shreds in a minute. Stories circulated of those who'd tried, of the gangs who'd forced it on a despised victim, of the willing brick somewhere in the wall who encouraged it, got it round the clock and asked for more.

I survived the meal in silence. Better for the moment to truck on my reputation as a dangerous enigma than expose it with feeble protests. The fact of my unfair treatment wouldn't inspire any more sympathy from the softer criminals than it had from Jimmy Shand, the brick in the hole. I shrugged away comments, the thrown bits of rolled-up bread, and a hand on my knee, and did more or less as they predicted by retreating to my cell. The television room, the gym, the other common spaces were challenges to be met some other day.

"Shoecat cheese!" said John Jones. "Beefshoe crab!"

"Quiet you goddamn nut!"

"If you'd seen it you wouldn't laugh," said Jones ominously.

They were expecting me in the upper bunk. My father had been listening to Billy Lancing tell an extended story about a hustle gone bad in western Kansas, while they both fended off Jones.

"Nick Marra," said my father.

I was pleased, thinking he recognized me now. But he only said, "How'd you get sent up, Marra?" and I understood that he didn't remember his own last name.

"Robbery," I said. I still responded automatically with the minimum. My crime didn't get more impressive with the addition of details.

"You're in a rush?" said Floyd.

"What?"

"You haven't got all day? You're going somewhere? Tell your story, kid."

We talked. He drew the tale of my crime and arrest out of me. He and Billy Lancing laughed when I got to the collision with the police cruiser, and Floyd said, "Fucking cop was probably jerking off with the other hand."

"He'll be telling it that way from now on," said Billy. "Won't you, Nick?"

"What?"

"Too good not to tell it like that," agreed Floyd.

And then, before I could tell him again that he was my father, he began to talk about his own crimes, and his punishments, before he was hardened. "—hadn't been sent upstairs to get the money he forgot, I woulda been killed in that crossfire like he was. 'Course my reward for living was the judge gave me all the years they wanted to give him—"

"Shit, you weren't more than a boy," said Billy.

"That's right," said Floyd. "Like this one."

"They all look like boys to me," said Billy. "Hey, man, tell him how you used to work for the prison godfather."

"Jesus, that's a long time ago," said Floyd, like he didn't want to get into it. "Long time ago . . . "

In fact he was just warming up.

The stories carried me out of myself, though I didn't exactly believe every word. I felt I'd been warned that embellishments were not only possible but likely. Floyd and Billy showed me that prison stories were myths, rendered in individual voices. What mattered were the universals, the telling.

I'd been using my story to show a connection between myself and Floyd, but the bricks weren't interested in connections. Billy and Floyd might have been accomplices in the job that got them sent up or they might never have met; either way they were now lodged catty-corner to one another forever, and the stories they told wouldn't change it, wouldn't change anything. The stories could only entertain, and get them attention from the living prisoners. Or fail to.

So I let go of trying to make Floyd admit that he was my father, for the moment. It was enough to try to understand it myself.

On the way back from dinner Lonely Boy and two others followed me back to my cell. The hall was eerily empty, every adjoining cell abandoned. I learned later that such moments were no accident, but well orchestrated. The three men twisted my arms back, pushed me into the toilet stall, out of sight of the wall, and pulled down my pants.

I will not describe them or give them names.

What they did to me took a long time.

Lonely Boy stroked the nape of my neck all through the ordeal. What they did was seldom tender, but he never stopped stroking the small hairs of my neck and talking to me. His words were all contradictions, and I soon stopped listening to them. The sound was the point anyway, a kind of cooing interspersed with jagged accusations. Rhythm and counterpoint; Lonely Boy was teaching me about my help-lessness, and the music of his words was a hook to help me remember. "Little special boy, special one. Why are you the special one? What did they choose you for? They pick you out for me? They send me a lonely one? You supposed be a spy here, you want to in-fil-trate? How are you gonna spend your lonely days? You gonna think of me? I know I been thinking of you. This whole place is thinking of you. They'll kill you if I don't watch out for you. I'm your pro-tec-tor now—"

When I finally was alone I crawled into the lower bed and turned away from the wall. But I heard Ivan Detbar's voice from above. He made sure he was heard.

"You don't have to go looking to find the top dog on the floor. The top dog finds you, that's what makes him what he is. He finds you and he's not afraid."

"Shit," said Billy Lancing.

"That's who you've got to take," said Detbar. "You've got to get on him like *thunder*. There is no other way."

"Shit," said Billy again. "First thing I learned in the joint is a virgin asshole's nothing to die for. It doesn't make the list."

Floyd wasn't talking.

Graham and another guard took me into an office the next day, an airless room on the interior.

"Okay," he said.

"Okay what?"

"Are you doing what we told you?"

"Talking? You didn't tell me anything more than that."

"Don't be smart. Your father trusts you?"

"Everything's great," I said. "So why don't you tell me what this is all about." I didn't bother to tell him that Floyd didn't agree that he was my father, that we hadn't even established that after almost three days of talk.

I was feeling oddly jaunty, having grasped the depths of my situation. And I wasn't all that impressed with Graham on his own. There wasn't anything he could take away from me.

I wanted more information, and I suspected I could get it.

"There's time for that," said Graham.

"I don't think so. All this weird attention is going to get me killed. They think I'm a spy for you, or they don't know what to think. I'm not going to be alive long enough for you to use me."

I wasn't interested in telling him about the previous night. I knew enough to know that it wouldn't improve anything for me. The problem was mine alone. I didn't know whether I was ever going to confront Lonely Boy, but if I did, it would be on prison terms. My priority now was to understand what they wanted from me and my father.

"You're exaggerating the situation," said Graham.

"I'm not. Tell me what this is about or I'll ask Floyd."

Graham considered me. I imagine I looked different than when they first dragged me out of the hole. I felt different.

He made a decision. "You'll be brought back here. Don't do anything you'll regret."

The other guard took me back to my cell.

It was a few hours later that I was standing in front of the man who didn't introduce himself the first time. He didn't again. He just told me to sit down. Graham stood to one side.

"Do you know the name Carl Allen Hemphill?" asked the man.

"Carl," I said, surprised.

"Very good. Have you been speaking with your father about him?"

"What? No."

"Did you know he was a prisoner here?"

"No." I'd heard he'd been a prisoner. But I didn't know he'd been a prisoner in the prison built of human bricks. "He's here now?" Somehow I was stupid enough to yearn for an old friend inside the prison, to imagine they were offering a reunion.

"He's dead."

I received it as a small, blunt impact somewhere in my

192

stomach. It was muffled by the distance of years since I'd seen him, and by my situation, my despair. Sure he was dead, I thought. Around here everything is dead. But why tell me?

"So?" I said.

"Listen carefully, Nick. Do you remember the unsuccessful attempt on the President's life?"

"Sure."

"The assassin, the man that was killed—that was your friend."

"Bottmore," I said, confused. "Wasn't his name Richard Bottmore, or Bottomore, something like that—"

"That wasn't his real name. His real name was Carl Allen Hemphill."

"That's crazy." I'd barely begun to struggle with the notion of Carl's having been here, his death. The assassination was too much, like being suddenly asked to consider the plight of the inhabitants of the moon. The point of this conversation, the answers I was seeking, seemed to whirl further and further out of my reach. "Why would he want to do that?"

"We'd very much like the answer to that question, Nick." He smiled at me as though he'd said enough, and thought I could take it from there. For a blind, hot second I wanted to kill him. Then he spoke again.

"He did his time quietly. Library type, loner. Nothing that was any indication. He was released five months before the attempt."

"And?"

"He had your cell."

"That's what this is about?" It seemed upside down. Was he saying that my real connection with Floyd didn't interest them, wasn't the point?

"Floyd hasn't said anything?"

"I told you no."

This time it was the man at the desk who lit a cigarette, and he didn't offer me one. I waited while he finished lighting it and arranging it in his mouth.

When he spoke again, his expression was oddly distanced. It was the first time I felt I might not have his full attention. "Hemphill left some papers behind. Very little of any value to the investigation so far. But he mentioned your father. It's one of the only interesting leads we have.

"The people I work with believe Hemphill didn't act alone. The more we dig up on his background, the more we glimpse the outlines of a conspiracy. You understand, I can't tell you any more than that or I'll be putting you in danger."

His self-congratulatory reluctance to "put me in danger" put a bad taste in my mouth. "You're crazy," I said. "Floyd doesn't know anything about that."

"Don't try to tell me my job," said the man behind the desk. "Hemphill left a list of targets. This is not a small matter. It was your father's name in his book. Not some other name. Floyd Marra."

I felt a stirring of jealousy. Carl and my father, my father who wouldn't admit he was. "Why don't you talk to Floyd yourself?"

"We tried. He played dumb."

What if he is dumb, I wanted to say. I was trying to square these bizarre revelations with the face in the wall, the brick I'd conversed with for the past three days. Trying to picture them questioning Floyd and coming away with the impression that he was holding something vital back.

"Can't bug the wall, either," said Graham. "Fuckers warn each other. Whisper messages."

"The wall doesn't like us, Nick. It doesn't cooperate. Floyd isn't stupid. He knows who he's talking to. That's why we need you."

He doesn't know who he's talking to when he's talking to me, I wanted to say.

"I'll ask him about Carl for you," I said. I knew I would, for my own reasons.

"Crabshit fish," interrupted Jones. "That's a hell of a thing."

It nearly expressed the way I felt. "He almost started a war," I said to Floyd, trying harder to make my point.

"He was a good kid," said Floyd. "Like you."

"Scared like you, too," said Ivan Detbar.

I had to remind myself that the bricks didn't see television or read newspapers, that Floyd hadn't lived in the world for over thirteen years. The President didn't mean anything to him. Not that he did to me.

"How'd you know him?" said Floyd. "Cellmates?"

It was an uncharacteristic question. It acknowledged human connections, or at least it seemed that way to me. Something knotted in my stomach. "We were in school together, junior high," I said. "He was my best friend."

"Best friend," Floyd echoed.

"After you were put here," I said, as though the framework was understood. "Otherwise you would have known him. He was around the house all the time. Mom—Doris— used to—"

"Get this cell rat," said Floyd. "Talking about the past. His mom."

"Heh," said Billy Lancing.

"That's a lot like that other one," said Ivan Detbar. "What's his name, Hemphill. He was a little soft."

195

"No wonder they were best friends," said Floyd. "Mom. Hey Billy, how's your *mom?*"

"Don't know," said Billy. "Been a while."

Now I hated him, though in fact he'd finally restored me to some family feeling. He'd caused me to miss Doris. She knew who I was, would remember me, and remember Carl as I wanted him remembered, as a boy. And besides, I knew her. I didn't remember my father and I was sick of pretending.

What's more, in hating him, I recalled an old feeling of trying to share in Doris's hatred of him, not in support but because I'd envied her the strength of the emotion. She'd known Floyd, she had a person to love or hate. I had nothing, I had no father. There was the void of my memories and there was this scarred brick, and between them somewhere a real man had existed, but that real man was forever inaccessible to me. I wanted to go back to Doris, I wanted the chance to tell her that I hated him now too. I felt that somehow I'd failed her in that.

I was crying, and the bricks ignored me, I thought.

"Hemphill sure got screwed, didn't he?" said Billy.

"The kid couldn't take this place," said Ivan Detbar.

"But he was a good kid," said Floyd.

"Wasn't his fault, something tripped him up bad," said Billy. "Something went down."

Through my haze of emotions—jealousy, bitterness, desolation—I realized they were offering me a warning, and perhaps some sort of apology.

The talk of Carl made me remember my assignment.

"You guys talked a lot?" I said.

"I guess," said Floyd.

"Nothing else to do," said Billy. "Less I'm missing something. Floyd, you been holding out on me?"

"Heh," said Floyd.

"There wasn't any talk about what he was going to do when he got out?" I asked. My task might be only an absurd joke, but at the moment it was all I had.

"I don't hear you talking about what you're going to do when you get out, and you're only doing a three-year stretch," said my father.

"What?"

"That's the last thing you want to think about now, isn't it? Maybe when you get a little closer."

"I don't understand."

"That poor kid was here at the start of ten years," said Floyd. "Hey, Billy. You ever meet a guy at the start of a long stretch wants to talk about what he's gonna do when he *finishes*?"

"Not unless he's planning a break, like Detbar here. Hah."

"I'll do it, too," said Detbar. "And I ain't taking you with me, you motherfucker."

"But he got out," I said, confused. "Hemphill, I mean."

"Yeah, but all of a sudden," said Floyd. "He *thought* he was doing ten years."

"Why all of a sudden?" I said. "What happened?"

"Somebody gave him a deal. They had a job for him. Let him out if he did it."

"Yeah, but that just made him sorrier," said Billy. "He was one screwed-up cat."

"He was okay," said Floyd. "He just had to tough it out. Like Marra here."

It was as disconcerting to hear him use the last name—as though it had nothing to do with him—as it was to be linked again and again with Carl. The dead grown-up would-be assassin and the lost child friend. It drew me out of my little investigation and back to my own concerns.

I couldn't keep from trying again. "Floyd?" What I wanted was so absurdly simple.

"Uh?"

"I want to talk to you about Doris Thayer," I said. I wasn't going to use the word *mom* again soon.

"Tell me about her again."

"She was my mother, Floyd."

"I felt that way about her too," said Floyd. "Like a mother. She really was something." He wasn't being funny this time. His tone was humble. It meant something to him, just not what I wanted it to mean.

"She was really my mother, Floyd. And you're my father."

"I'm nobody's father, Marra. What do I look like?"

That wasn't a question I wanted to answer. I'd learned that I didn't even want to watch his one eye blink, his lips work to form words. I always turned slightly away. If I concentrated on his voice, he seemed more human, more real.

"Come on, Marra, tell me what you see," said Floyd.

I realized the face of the brick was creeping into my patched-together scraps of memory. For years I'd tried to imagine him in the house, to play back some buried image of him visiting, or with Doris. Now when I tried, I saw the empty socket, the flattened skull, the hideous naked stone.

I swallowed hard, gathering my nerve, and pressed on. "How long ago did you come here?"

"Been a million years."

"Million years ago the dogshit bird ruled the earth," said John Jones. "Crawled outta the water, all over the place. It's *evolutionary*."

"Like another life to me," said Floyd, ignoring him. His voice contained an element of yearning. I told myself I was getting somewhere.

"Okay," I said. "But in that other life, could you have been somebody's father?"

A shadow fell across the floor of my cell. I looked up. Lonely Boy was leaning against the bars, hanging there with his arms up, his big fingers inside and in the light, the rest of him in darkness.

"Looking for daddy?" he said.

The next day I told Graham I wanted another meeting. The man who never introduced himself was ready later that afternoon. I was getting the feeling he had a lot of time on his hands.

His expression was boredom concealing disquiet, or maybe the reverse. "Talk," he said.

"Floyd doesn't really know anything. He's never even heard of the assassination attempt. I can't even get him to focus on that."

"That's hard to believe, under the circumstances."

"Well, start believing. You have to understand, Floyd doesn't think about things that aren't right in front of him anymore. His world is—small. Immediate." Suddenly I felt that I was betraying my father, describing him like an autistic child, when what I meant was, *He's been built into a wall and he doesn't even know who I am*.

It didn't seem right that I should have to explain it to the men responsible. But the man behind the desk still inspired in me a queasy mixture of defiance and servility. All I said was, "I think I might have something for you anyway."

"Ah," he said. "Please."

I was going to tell him that he was right, there had been a conspiracy, and that Carl had been recruited from inside. An insipid fantasy ran in my mind, that he would jump up and clap me on my back, tell me I'd cracked the case, deputize me, free me. But as I opened my mouth to speak, the man across the desk leaned forward, somehow too pleased already, and I stopped. I thought involuntarily: *What I'm about to tell him, he knows.* And I didn't speak.

I have often wondered if I saved my own life in that moment. The irony is that I nearly threw it away in the next. Or rather, caused it to be thrown.

"Yes?" he said. "You were going to say?"

"Floyd remembered Carl talking about some—group," I said, inventing. "Some kind of underground organization."

He raised his eyebrows at this. It was not what he was expecting. It seemed to take him a moment to find his voice. "Tell me about this—organization."

"They're called the Horseshoe Crabs," I said. "I don't really know more than that. Floyd just isn't interested in politics, I guess. But anyway, that should be enough to get you started."

"The Horseshoe Crabs."

"Yes."

"An *in-prison* underground?"

"No," I said quickly. "Something from before." I was a miserable liar.

I must have been looking at the floor. I didn't even see him leave his seat and come around the desk, let alone spot the fury accumulating in his voice or expression. He was just suddenly on me, my collar in his hands, his face an inch from mine. "You're fucking with me, Nick," he said.

"No."

"I can tell. You think I can't tell when I'm being fucked by an *amateur?*" He shoved me to the floor. I knocked over a trash basket as I fell. I looked at Graham. He just stood impassively watching, a foot away but clearly beyond appeal.

"What are the Horseshoe Crabs?" said the man. "Is Floyd a Horseshoe Crab?"

"He just said the name, that Carl used it. That's all I know."

"Stand up."

I got on my feet, but my knees were trembling. Rightly, since he immediately knocked me to the floor again.

Then Graham spoke. "Not here."

"Fine," said the man, through gritted teeth. "Upstairs."

They took me in an elevator up to the top floor, hustling me ahead of them roughly, making a point now. As they ran me through corridors, Graham pushing ahead and opening gates, living inmates jeered maliciously from their cells. They made a kind of wall themselves, fixed in place and useless to me as I went by. Graham unlocked the last door and we went up a stairway to the roof and burst out into the astonishing light of the sky. It was white, gray really, but absolutely blank and endless. It was the first sky I'd seen in two weeks. I thought of how Floyd hadn't seen it in thirteen years, but I was too scared to be outraged for him.

"Grab him," the man said to Graham. "Don't let him do it himself."

The roof was a worksite; they were always adding another level, stacking newly hardened bricks to form another floor. The workers were the first-timers, the still-soft. But there was nobody here now, just the disarray of discontinued work. A heap of thin steel dowels waiting to be run through the stilled bodies, plastic barrels of solvent for melting their side surfaces together into a wall. In the middle of the roof was a pallet of new human bricks, maybe twenty-five or thirty of them, under a battened-down tarp. In the roar of the wind I could just make out the sound of their keening.

Graham and the man from behind the desk took me by my arms and walked me to the nearest edge. Crossing that open distance made me know again how huge the prison was. I kept my head down, protecting my ears from the cold whistle of the wind and my eyes from the empty sky.

The new story was two bricks high at the edge we reached. The glossy top side of the bricks had been grooved and torn with metal rasps so the bond would take. Graham held me by my arms and bent me over the short wall, just as Lonely Boy and the others had bent me over the toilet.

"Take a look," said the man.

"Looks like rain to me," said one of the nearby bricks chattily.

My view was split by a false horizon: the dark mass of the sheer face of the prison receding earthward below the dividing line, and above it the empty acres of concrete and broken glass. From the thirty-two-story height the ground sparkled like the sea viewed from an airplane.

Graham jammed me harder against the rough top of the bricks, and tilted me further towards the edge. I grunted, and watched a glob of my own drool tumble into the void.

"I hate to be fucked with," said the man. "I don't have time for that."

I made a sound that wasn't a word.

"Maybe we'll chop your father out of the wall and throw you both off," said the man. "See which hits the ground first."

I managed to think how odd it was to threaten a man in prison with the open air, the ultimate freedom. It was the reverse of the hole, all space and light. But it served their purpose just as well. Something I reflected on later was how just about anything could be turned to serve purposes like this.

"What are the Horseshoe Crabs?" he said.

I'd already forgotten how this all resulted from my idiotic gambit. "There are no Horseshoe Crabs," I gasped.

"You're lying to me."

"No."

"Throw him over, Graham."

Graham pressed me disastrous inches closer. My shirt and some of the skin underneath caught on the shredded upper surface of the wall.

"You're not telling me why I should spare you," said the man.

"What?" I said, gulping at the cold wind.

"You're not telling me why I should spare you."

"I'll tell you everything you want to know," I said.

Graham pulled me back.

"Are you lying to me again?" said the man.

"No. Let me talk to Floyd. I'll find out whatever you want."

"I want to know about the Horseshoe Crabs."

"Yes."

"I want to know anything he knows. You're my listening device, direct from him to me. I don't want any more noise in the signal. Do you understand?"

I nodded.

"Take him back, Graham. I'm going to have a cigarette."

Graham took me to my cell. I climbed into the top bunk and lay still until my trembling faded.

"The kid's getting ready to make his move," said Ivan Detbar.

"You think so?" said Floyd.

It was dinner hour. Inmates were shambling through the corridor towards Mess Nine.

My thoughts were black, but I had a small idea.

It seemed to me that one of my problems might solve the other. The way Graham had said "not here" to the man behind the desk made me think that the man's influence might not extend very far within the prison, however extensive and malignant it was in the world at large. I had never seen him command anyone besides Graham. Graham was in charge of my block, but the trip upstairs had made me remember the immensity of the prison.

My idea was simple, but it required physical bravery, not my specialty to this point. The cafeteria was the right place for it. With so many others at hand I might survive.

"Floyd," I said.

"Yeah?"

"What if you weren't going to see me anymore? Would that change anything?"

"What are you getting at?"

"Anything you'd want to say?"

"Take care, nice knowing ya," he said.

"How about 'Don't do anything I wouldn't do'?" said Billy Lancing.

Floyd and Billy laughed at that. I let them laugh. When they were done I said, "One last question, Floyd."

"Shoot."

I'd thought I was losing interest, growing numb. I guess in the long sense I was. But I still had to press him a little harder before the opportunity passed. "Did you know your father?" I asked.

"You're asking me—what? My old man?" Floyd's eye rolled, like he thought his father had appeared somewhere in the cell.

"You knew him?"

"If I could get my hands around the neck of that son of a bitch—"

"You talk big, Floyd," said Ivan. "What about when you had your chance?"

"Fuck you," said Floyd. "I was a kid. I barely knew that motherfucker."

"The Motherfuck Dog," said John Jones. "He lives under the house—"

The tears were on my face again, and without choosing to do it I was beating my fist against the wall, against Floyd's petrified body. Once, twice, then it was too painful to go on. And I don't think he noticed.

I got down from the bunk. I had another place for the fury to go, a place where it might have a use. I only had to get myself to that place before I thought twice.

Dinner was meatballs and mashed potatoes covered with steaming grayish gravy. I took two cups of black coffee aboard my tray as well. I turned out of the food line and located Lonely Boy, sitting with his seconds at a table on the far side of the crowded room. Before I could think again I headed for them.

"Hey, lonely boy, you want to sit?"

I flung the tray so it spilled on all three of them. I was counting on that to slow the other two; all my attention would be on Lonely Boy. I knew I'd lose any fight that was a contest of strategy or guile, lose it badly, that my only chance was blind instantaneous rage. So I went in with my hands instead of picking up a fork or some other weapon. For my plan to work, Lonely Boy had to live. With what I knew was in me to unleash, however, his life seemed as much at risk as mine.

They pulled us apart before very long, but I'd already gotten my hands around his throat and begun hitting his head against the table, rhythmic revenge. One of his seconds had taken a tray and lashed open my scalp with it, and my blood was running into my opponent's eyes, and my own, and mixing with the coffee on the table. The voices around us roared.

Back in the hole for the night that followed, I screamed, bled, shat. I shoved the morning tray back out as it was coming through the slot. I attacked the men that came for me. How much was pretense I can't really say. Maybe none. When they got me into the shower I calmed down somewhat. I didn't feel human, though. I felt mercenary and cold, like frozen acid.

They put six stitches in my scalp in the prison hospital and led me to another, larger office, with more file cabinets and chairs, more ashtrays. Graham was there, with two other men. One of the others did the talking.

Those others were my margin, I knew. My glint of light.

The one who spoke asked me about the fight.

"If I'm put back in the block with him, one of us will have to die," I said simply.

I could see a look of satisfaction on the face of the other of the two men, not Graham. I assumed Lonely Boy had been trouble to this man before. I assumed too that I'd done damage. I smiled back at this man, and I smiled at Graham.

Graham kept his face impassive.

The man who was talking explained to me that Lonely Boy was an established presence on block nine, that he had more support than might have been apparent—did I understand that?

"Move me upstairs," I said. "As far away as possible. If I see him again, I'll have to kill him."

The one who was talking told me that I'd likely find men like Lonely Boy wherever I went in the prison.

Nobody said the word *rape*.

"I'll never be in this position again," I said. "I can promise you that. Nobody will ever be permitted to make the mistake he made."

The man raised his eyebrows. The other one, the smiling one, smiled. Graham sat.

"Just move me," I said.

"We don't let prisoners make our decisions for us, Mr. Marra," said Graham.

"Your unusual handling put me at a disadvantage in the situation, Mr. Graham. If you keep me on block nine, I intend to be treated like the other prisoners."

The man who had been talking turned and looked at Graham, and in that moment I knew I would be transferred.

"Unusual handling?" said the man who'd smiled. He directed the question at me, but it was Graham who spoke.

"He presents unique difficulties," he said. "His father is in the prison. In the wall. I thought it was better to address it directly."

I took a leaf from Floyd's book. It was pure improvisation, but my skills at lying were improving rapidly. "He isn't my father."

The smiling man made an inquiring face.

"He knew my mother, I guess. But she told me later he wasn't my father. He's just some guy. Just another brick to me."

The smiling man smiled at Graham. "This doesn't seem to me to require special treatment."

"I had the impression—" Graham began.

The smiling man laughed. "Apparently mistaken, Graham."

Graham laughed along.

Graham never spoke to me again, though I lived in fear of some reprisal. I would see him moving through the corridors with the men in charge of my block or other blocks and think he was about to point a finger at me and say, "Marra, come with me," but he never did. I don't think he cared enormously. It might have been some relief to him to be able to say to the man behind the desk that I'd slipped away. Graham was a man with a difficult job and dealing with the man behind the desk was clearly not an easy part of it.

I never saw the man behind the desk again.

He was a sadist and an idiot. The two were not mutually exclusive, I understood after that day on the roof. The agency or service he worked for had assigned him the task of tracing a conspiracy he was a member of himself. Sending me in to question my father was just ritual activity. He might have been curious to know whether Hemphill had talked about what was happening to him, but he wasn't worried. He hadn't even bothered to wire the cell, or he'd have known how I came up with *horseshoe crabs*. Until I'd panicked him, triggered his paranoia with that bluff, he was just making a show of activity by torturing me. And keeping himself entertained, I suppose, killing time on an absurd assignment.

The only deeper explanation was that I'd become a kind of stand-in for Carl, the other young prisoner they'd had in their grasp. He'd been theirs, for a time, and then he twisted loose, became history. I don't know if what he did was a disastrous perversion of their plans, or whether it served them, but I sensed that either way they experienced a loss. The mechanism of control was more precious than any outcome. I'd become the new instrument, the new site where control was enacted. Until I broke the spell.

As for Carl himself, I hadn't learned much about the tortured prisoner and would-be assassin, and I didn't have any interest in trying to learn more. The image of my thirteen-year-old friend had been obliterated without anything taking its place. I didn't object. He was just a ghost now, and there were plenty of more substantial ghosts available, in the wall.

I became another prisoner in a cell, living out my hours, hoarding my grudges, protecting my back. I spent days in the weight room, years in the television room. I told lies to make the time pass. The rest of my story was no different from anyone else's, so in the telling I made it as different as I could. I learned to use the phrase *fuck the wall*, though like a million other cowards I never tried it.

I didn't see my father again until a week before I left the prison, when I was granted a minute in my old cell.

Billy Lancing was still the same. He looked me over when I came in and said, "Marra?"

"Yeah."

"I remember you. Where'd you go?"

"Upstairs."

"Well, I remember you."

I climbed up into the top bunk.

Ivan Detbar was dead, his eyes stilled. I recognized it instantly by now. John Jones was still raving, but more quietly, not looking for an audience anymore.

My father was still alive, if that's the word for it, but someone had pried out his other eye, splintering the stony bridge of his nose in the process.

His mouth was moving, but nothing was coming out.

"Floyd's not good," said Billy.

I went over and put my hand on him. He couldn't feel it, of course. I was touching my father, but it didn't matter to either of us.

I wondered if it was Graham or the man behind the desk who'd removed the eye, in some offhand act of revenge. It could as easily have been a living prisoner, someone in that top bunk who'd taken offense at too much attention, or at some joke.

Floyd, like Billy, had listened fairly well. That was the only real difference between him and the hundreds of other bricks I'd met by that time. What had happened between him and Carl was absurdly simple, but the man behind the desk was puzzled, because it wasn't supposed to happen to an assassin-in-training, or to a human brick. They'd become friends. Floyd had expressed his dim, blundering sympathy, and Carl had listened, and been drawn out of his fear.

Which was more or less all Floyd had done with me.

Had he pretended not to know me, pretended not to make the connection between my stories, my family history, and his? I'd stopped wondering pretty quickly. I had more immediate problems, which was part of his point, I think, if he was making one.

Bricks only face one direction.

I let my hand slip from the wall, and left the cell.

Sleepy People

He was no danger to her. Judith Map felt that immediately. He lay on the porch, one arm flung out across her doormat, obscuring the word WELCOME. She'd come home late from work. The street was silent, apart from crickets chirping and a far-off siren. She could see his chest rise and fall calmly. She turned her key in the door and stepped past him.

Inside, she switched on the porch light, and looked at him through the glass pane at the top of the door. He wore jeans and workboots, and a tee-shirt which read QUICK'S LITTLE ALASKA. It was the name of the bar at the corner where her street met Schermerhorn Avenue, three blocks away. It was called Little Alaska because of the air conditioning.

A car pulled into a drive up the street, headlights flaring over the porch where he lay. Another of her neighbors coming home. The street led nowhere, and the only cars that went past were cars that belonged to houses there. Nobody on her street walked except Judith. But the man on the porch must have walked, or been carried. From the bar, she guessed.

She opened the door and lifted his arms and shoulders from underneath and dragged him across the threshold. His head lolled. The carpet at the entry bunched under his back, so that she had to nudge it away with her toe. She grunted, heard her own rough breath. His was still calm. She draped his arms over his stomach, and stepped out onto the porch. No one was watching. She shut the door.

She dragged him a little farther into the room, to the space between the sofa and the coffee table. She felt a little trickle of sweat under her arms. It was enough, she'd moved him enough. She went to the kitchen and filled a glass with water. When she went back in to look at him she was struck by the beauty of his features at rest. She felt she understood him. Though she didn't understand how he had gotten to her porch.

She'd heard about the sleepy people, but she'd never met one before.

She climbed over the back of the sofa and sat with her legs crossed and peered down at him. Her heart was beating fast. She wasn't frightened. She wondered if she should bring him a blanket, then remembered that the sleepy people conserved energy, kept themselves warm. He'd been on the porch, after all. Though really this was the kind of night where it was as warm outdoors as in. A perfectly calm night, as if it had settled itself around his sleeping body. She was the only thing agitated, her breath unsteady. But she wasn't frightened.

Should she move him back to the porch? He might have wanted to be there. He fit nicely between the couch and the coffee table, though. She climbed over the back again, and went to her bedroom door. From that vantage he was completely out of sight. What if someone were looking for him? It would be someone from the bar, from Little Alaska. They might have left him here just because they couldn't carry him anymore, intending to come back. Certainly her neighbors wouldn't leave a sleepy man on her porch. But the people in the bar, the militia, never left the bar. She tangled again in the mystery of his arrival on her porch.

It didn't matter. She was suddenly exhausted. She pictured herself stretched out on the sofa, alongside him but perched above. It was absurd, she decided, and thrust it aside. She went into the bedroom and locked the door, quickly. That too was absurd; she might as well have left him on the porch. It was as though she wanted to abdicate the house to him and reduce her own space to the single room.

She unlocked the door, and left it ajar. She could see the back of the sofa from her bed. She could hear him breathe.

She didn't dream, but woke thinking of him. She got out of bed to check; he was still there. His arm was threaded through the legs of the coffee table. She pictured him flinging his arms, gesticulating in the night. Otherwise he lay there exactly as she'd left him. She went to the kitchen and made herself coffee.

When she was ready for work she lifted his shoulders again and dragged him around the other side of the sofa, and back out to the porch. She didn't want to lock him inside. What else she wanted wasn't clear, but she shouldn't lock him inside. *Her back grew strong from moving him daily*, she imagined reading in an eighteenth-century novel. His boots clunked, one after another, over the doorjamb. She propped his head and shoulders slightly, just because it seemed righter for day-time. Anyone could see him from the street.

There were only two other people left in her office, Tom and Eva. There had been six people working there when she started, two years before. It was telephone work. They were collecting information. The information was highly specific: the price of carpets and hardware, the cost of garbage collection and plumbing repair. The rent board had hired them to study the legitimacy of an appeal by the commission of landlords for a cost-related increase in fixed rents. She conducted phone interviews with suppliers, repairmen, and landlords picked at random. They weren't necessarily the landlords who'd requested the increase, and they didn't always understand the questions she asked.

Halfway through the morning she called Eva's cubicle instead of the next number on her list.

"A sleepy man came to my house," she said.

"Sleeping?" said Eva.

"He's sleeping, yes. But sleepy, also. One of the sleepy people."

"Do you have any houseplants?" said Eva, whispering.

"Yes."

"They make plants grow," said Eva. "If you put them in the same room. Also sharpen razor blades."

"Really?"

"That's all I know. I better go, I've got a call."

"Thanks," said Judith.

"Sure. I think you have to put the plants pretty close to them."

"Okay."

She went back to work. She knew that Eva and Tom spoke on the phone between their cubicles all the time. Tom and Eva were in love, she guessed. They never spoke in front of her.

She walked home a little early. He was still there, propped beside the door where she'd left him. She realized she'd been holding her breath. The evening sun cast the whole porch in yellow glaze, and the sleepy man seemed to her like a diver figurine resting at the bottom of a golden aquarium. She almost didn't want to intrude. But she went past him, let herself in, dropped her keys on the sofa. There was half a casserole in the refrigerator; she moved it to the oven.

She poured herself a glass of wine to go with the leftovers, and sat drinking and just nibbling, poking at the food. Through the window the porch framed a sunset that glowed and died like an ember. The street was very quiet. He was still outside, his head just below the window frame.

A dog barked. It was night. She thought of how it wasn't safe to leave him out all night. There were the people that roamed making trouble, the dinosaurs. They sometimes found this street, though it led nowhere particular, though it was just one of so many residential streets. She'd heard them, and seen her neighbors' torn-up lawns, wrecked mailboxes. A sleepy person would be a natural target for the dinosaurs.

Every sleepy person should have someone to take care of them, she thought. That seemed simple enough.

She went out and lifted his shoulders and dragged him inside. This time she got him up onto the sofa, first sitting him against it, then hoisting him up like a baby into a car seat, finally swinging his legs up so that he turned and sank against the pillows. She closed the curtains and got her wineglass and brought it over and sat with him, perching her buttocks on the lip of cushion left free. The margin wasn't enough, and she slid down to the floor between the sofa and the coffee table. She'd taken his place.

She emptied her glass and put it on the coffee table. Outside, the dog barked again.

She turned in the little coffin-like space and was faced with his middle. His Little Alaska tee-shirt had bunched up where she'd gripped him under his shoulders. His stomach was almost black with hair. It whorled in a devilish vee in and out of his navel and into his jeans. She was very close, having turned there. She propped herself with her elbows on the coffee table. He wasn't fat but the jeans were tight on his hips, and there was a pinkish imprint of seam where they pinched his flesh. His fly was fastened with steel buttons. She undid the first. She could smell him a little. Her mouth tasted like wine.

The buttons had worn out their buttonholes. She only had to nudge them apart. His penis was beating slightly, like it had a little heart of its own. She covered it with her hand, then put her lips to her knuckles. His hair tickled her nose. Under her hand his penis was twitching, growing in little throbs. His chest rose and fell as steadily as before.

She pushed the backing cushions off the sofa to make room to fit her knee, and moved his arms up above his head, so that he resembled some sculpture she'd seen, a saint or slave carved in marble. But with stubble. Saint Stubble of Little Alaska, she thought. His erection was taut against his stomach now, the dewy pink head nestled in his black hair.

She slipped out of her underwear and clambered on top, then reached down and placed him with her hand. She was very wet. He sighed. She imagined that he was pretending to be asleep. But he wasn't, really. She moved slowly, keeping him inside. The backs of her thighs were a little cold.

She brought herself to orgasm, bracing her other hand against his collarbone, not hurrying. She pitched forward. He grunted gently. Outside the dog was barking. She slid to the side and then, knees a bit tangled in her stockings and skirt, to the floor below him again.

She daubed at them both with her underwear, and buttoned him up. She stood and pulled her skirt up and it was as if nothing had happened, except her smeared underwear was on the floor and she felt a coolness and a trickling on the inside of her thighs. She ran a bath. Then she went out to him again and arranged his tee-shirt so it covered his stomach, and fit his arms back at his sides.

Something was wrong. The more she restored him, the deader he looked, as if she were a mortician. She moved him with difficulty to the easy chair, which was an improvement. It seemed to put more of an end to the affair. Then, a little guiltily, as though it should have been the first thing she'd done on coming home, she gathered the houseplants. There were four of them, a fern, a spiderplant, a tall thing that was some kind of succulent, with fat, fleshy plumes, and a small fist-like cactus with white wisps of hair instead of spines. She arrayed them near his chair.

He slept on. She got into the bath.

When she got home from work the next day, the plants already seemed bigger, and the fern, the most flexible of the four, was definitely bent towards him, as if in the direction of sunlight. His position was changed too, his head tipped forward, chin on his chest, and his arms were folded. It gave him a decisive, even obstinate look. She put her things on the sofa and went into the kitchen.

After dinner she put on her coat again and went out onto the porch. The street was quiet. It was a cold night. It looked safe. She closed the door.

Perhaps the people in the bar would know something about the sleepy man.

Quick's Little Alaska was a perfect cube, like a children's block that had been disguised with scribbles of neon and daubs of graffiti and surrounded with Dumpsters and parked or abandoned cars so it could pass as a building. The cars on Schermerhorn Avenue raced by, oblivious. Judith herself didn't know anyone with a car anymore. Eva and Tom walked all the way downtown to work, like she did. Judith suspected the people inside Quick's, the militia, hadn't driven their cars, if they had cars, for a long time. The cars around the bar didn't look like they'd been started in a while. They all had cat footprints on the windshields and hoods.

It was chilly inside, as advertised. Everyone at the bar turned when she stepped through the door. Farther inside, at the cluster of tables, nobody seemed particularly interested. She recognized some of the faces, others were new. She took a deep breath and went to the bar.

The music playing was slurred and slow, a voice and a trumpet winding down like an uncranked engine.

The man working the bar was one she remembered from the last time she'd come in, years ago. He was the son of Quick, the owner. His hair was red, like his father's. He moved over to where she stood and cleared away an empty bottle. He obviously remembered her too. "What can I do you for, Judith?" he said. "Looking for someone?"

"Not exactly," she said. She knew that Quick's son meant someone in particular: John, who had been Judith's husband once. John was sitting in the back of the bar, at one of the tables. He was part of the militia now. He was a general. Judith tried not to look his way.

"Do you sell tee-shirts?" she said.

In answer Quick's son reached underneath the bar and pulled out a shirt identical to the one the sleepy man wore.

"Yes, that's it," she said.

"You want one?"

"No. There's a man—he had one. I was wondering if you knew him."

Quick's son didn't answer, but the man beside her at the bar turned and said, "Where'd you see him?"

He had a beard and was wearing a sweater with leather patches and the kind of hat she imagined men wore on fishing boats.

"He was sleeping on my porch," she said.

The bearded man raised his eyebrow and said, "Give the lady a drink, Red."

"She didn't order anything," said Quick's son.

"I don't need anything," Judith said. "Do you know the man, the one who was sleeping?"

The bearded man raised a finger and said, "Lieutenant?"

A woman a seat away from him rested her elbow on the bar and peered at him and Judith over the top of her half-glasses.

"Lady's looking for Danny-boy," said the bearded man.

"I'm not looking for him," Judith said quickly. "I wanted to know if he came from here." *Danny-boy*, she thought. If that was his name, if they meant the same person.

"Sure, sure," said the older woman. "We understand what you mean. Danny-boy giving you trouble?"

"No," said Judith. "So he was here? He lived in the bar?"

"He's Absent without Leave," said the bearded man. "It sounds like you have information concerning his where-abouts." He took a large finishing swallow of his drink. "Another like that, Red," he said to Quick's son, who was leaning on his side of the bar. "And don't listen in on privi-leged communication."

"Okay, okay," said Quick's son.

"Danny-boy's not in any trouble, is he?" said the older woman, removing her half-glasses. They were strung around her neck by a red cord and rested crookedly in her cleavage.

"No," said Judith again, a little confused. If anything, she was getting him into trouble by coming here.

"Sounds like he's found himself a woman," said the bearded man.

"Sergeant, we don't presume anything around here," said the older woman, the lieutenant. "We operate on the basis of verifiable fact."

Quick's son was still leaning in from his side of the bar, listening. They'd attracted another listener, too, a man with a cane, but no limp. He had hawk-like eyes and a gigantic nose. He stepped over and hung his cane on the bar.

"One of our scouts has been contacted, Admiral," said the woman, moving her eyebrows significantly.

The admiral turned and looked sharply at Judith, then reached out and pinched her chin. Judith jerked her head away. "Excellent disguise," said the man.

"Not her," said the lieutenant. "She's a civilian volunteer."

"Scout, that's a good one," said the sergeant. "Danny-boy couldn't scout the inside of his eyelids."

Judith didn't like agreeing with the abrasive sergeant, but she did want them to understand. "He's sleepy," she said.

"Who isn't?" said the admiral. "I'm interested in his findings, not his feelings." He turned and scowled across the bar. "Scotch, Quick."

Quick's son hurried to his bottles. Two other members of the militia joined them from the tables at the back of the room. A young woman in overalls, with a crewcut, and John, who had long ago been Judith's husband. "Hello, Judith," John said.

"General Map," said the admiral. "Hail."

"You joining our merry band?" John said to Judith, ignoring the admiral.

"I was just—I just had a question," said Judith.

"She's playing Betsy Crocker to a Benedict Arnold," said the sergeant sneeringly.

"Don't you mean Betsy *Ross?*" said the lieutenant.

Quick's son put a whiskey on the bar in front of the admiral, then opened two bottles of beer and handed them to the woman in overalls, who passed one to John. Quick's son still hadn't refilled the sergeant's glass, Judith noticed.

"Danny-boy?" said John to the lieutenant. She nodded sagely.

"He's taken up position on a porch," said the admiral, and then added, "As per my orders," and shot a fierce look at the sergeant.

Judith opened her mouth to say that he wasn't actually on the porch anymore, that he'd been moved inside. But she didn't speak.

"So what's the problem?" said John, his eyes on Judith.

"Communication is poor-to-nonexistent," said the admiral, with a hard look in his eyes.

"Snoring, however, is highly satisfactory," japed the sergeant.

"Admiral, why don't you buy the young lady a drink?" said the lieutenant. "I hate to see her empty-handed."

"It's fine," said Judith.

"Make it a round for the house," said the sergeant. "That's the only way I'll ever get a drink around here."

"We'll reestablish communication when we need to," said John to the admiral. "For the time being let's leave Danny-boy where he is. Deep in mufti."

The woman in overalls suddenly laughed.

"In mufti?" said the sergeant puzzledly.

"A round for the house," said John. "I'm buying."

"Mighty white of you, General," said the lieutenant. But John was already headed back to his table.

"Mighty white of you, General," echoed the sergeant in a mocking whine.

"Young lady, I wonder if perhaps you would accompany me to a booth?" said the admiral to Judith.

"No thank you," she said. "I have to go."

In another day the cactus had grown extra knobs, on the side that faced him. Almost like tumors, she thought. The needle-fur over the new growth was downy, like a baby's first hair. It was overweighted on that side now, and nearly tipping its pot. She turned it so the new growth faced away from him.

The other three had proliferated too. The spiderplant had cast new trailers over his ankle, and the fern and the succulent were both turned towards him, and thicker and shinier on his side. He was like King Arthur, she thought. The land, the crops, grew when he was well and died when he was sick. Or was it the other way? King Midas, maybe that was righter. Golden touch. She wanted him to have a title or rank, like the others from the bar. Danny-boy didn't seem enough.

Porch King. Arthur Midas, Porch King. Maybe she should move him out to the porch again.

Instead she moved the plants all a little farther away, then stood back and looked. She was embarrassed for him, somehow, in a cozy chair surrounded by the eager foliage. It was too feminine, not really kingly at all, let alone military. She thought of the famous painting of the Midwestern farmer parting the cattails to find the nude sleeping there. He was still as inappropriate, as unexpected as that. The plants seemed to make it worse.

If she took him and the plants out together to the porch, they would be camouflage, not decoration. But it was too cold; the fern would die. And she wanted him inside. So she took them away to their original spots in the house. They'd basked enough, and what was happening to the cactus didn't necessarily seem so healthy anyway. Denuded of the plants he looked dead again, but she had an idea.

In the closet was her television, on a rolling metal stand. She didn't watch it anymore. It had gone from all news about militias forming and dinosaurs to replaying old shows that weren't about anything at all. She rolled it out of the closet to a spot in front of his chair and plugged it in, set the volume low, and stepped behind it to watch him. Perfect. He was transformed, restored. The flickering glow seemed to animate his features. It reminded her of when she found him, that first day, on the porch.

She went to the closet and took out a large cardboard mailing tube. It was still marked with stamps and stickers. She put one end in his lap and pointed the other across his shoulder, and arranged his arms around it as though it were a rifle. She tipped his head forward a bit so he seemed more attentive. If the dinosaurs looked in her window, they would see him keeping watch, waiting. Though it was hard to see it really as a rifle; they would think he was holding a bazooka, a flame thrower. Or a cardboard tube.

Finished, she knelt and let her head rest against his knee briefly. His breathing was soft and steady, as always. He was a good sleeper, she thought. He was getting good sleep. She touched his thigh. It felt nice. But that part of their relationship had to wait, she decided. He shouldn't be undressed now, she shouldn't be thinking of that.

"He made the plants grow."

223

She'd just learned that in one shop 70-watt lightbulbs were selling for two dollars and fifty cents apiece, while in another shop, a few blocks away from the first, they cost almost ten dollars. Then she'd called Eva.

"They all do that, I told you."

"Do you—have you known a sleepy person?"

"Well—" Eva giggled.

Out of the corner of her eye Judith saw Tom go from his cubicle to the door of Eva's. "Just a sec," said Eva.

Judith could make out their talk, though Eva must have had her hand over the mouthpiece. "Who's on the phone?" said Tom.

"It's Judith. We're talking."

"Hurry up, I want to go to lunch."

Eva came back on the line. "I have to go," she said.

When she got home, Judith saw that the new growths on the cactus had sagged, like little deflated balloons. The hair on them was thin and disordered. She brought the cactus back into the living room and put it on the floor at his feet, in front of the television.

That night from her bedroom, just as she was drifting off to the sound of the voices on the television, she heard him pad to the bathroom and pee. The sound of his urine falling into the little pool went on forever, and the tone rose, as if he were filling the bowl completely. Finally it stopped, and there came the sound of the faucet, then a slapping and slurping noise that she decided meant he was drinking from his cupped hands. He left the bathroom without flushing the toilet.

In the morning she saw he'd gotten to his chair and retaken the tube into his arms, though he was holding it more like a pillow than a rifle, hugging it to his chest, his grizzled cheek resting against it. A little stream of drool was soaked into the cardboard. She restored the tube to rifle position, then turned the television off for the day.

The cactus had already reinflated nicely.

At work she found that her phone couldn't be used to call the other cubicles anymore.

They arrived while she was brushing her teeth before bed. She was in a robe. It was a warm night. His television was on now, a reassuring monotone of chatter. They broke the front window with a rock from the yard. When she came out of the bathroom to look, someone had a foot through the broken window, tangling in the blind, and someone else was pounding on the front door. She opened it, and they came at her.

It was a group of dinosaurs, five of them, three male and two female. They looked young, younger than dinosaurs looked in the news. She wondered if any of them were even twenty. The first two through the door grabbed her by the arms. One pulled her wet toothbrush from her hand and threw it under the table. The last stepped in and closed the door.

"Drop it," one of them yelled. His hair was fluffed into an enormous Afro, and he wore a pumpkin-colored satin jacket with a fluted waist and sleeves. He poked a small knife toward the sleepy man and said again, "Drop it." Another dinosaur, a teenage girl, dashed forward and jerked the cardboard tube out of the sleepy man's arms, releasing it to clatter to the floor beside his chair.

"He's asleep," said Judith.

Keeping the knife at waist-level, the dinosaur with the Afro squinted at the sleepy man. "Sure he is," he said. "Be rough with her. We'll see how he likes that."

"What?" said the teenage girl.

"Be rough with her," said the one with the Afro. "Don't make me tell you twice."

They threw Judith back against the sofa. Her robe was flung open, revealing her body to them. She was wearing panties, nothing else. She was conscious of her appendectomy scar. The teenage girl took the knife and perched at the other end, on the arm of the sofa. "Sit still," she said.

"Search for stuff," said the dinosaur with the Afro to the others.

"What stuff?" said one of the other dinosaurs.

"Shut up," said the dinosaur with the Afro. "You know what I mean."

The dinosaurs began tearing up the house, two in the bedroom, two in the kitchen. They cleared cabinets with a sweeping arm, dumped every drawer and container on the floor, then tipped each piece of furniture onto its front, away from the wall. It didn't seem to Judith that they were really searching for anything, more like a ritual destruction. Even for that it was halfhearted.

The dinosaur with the Afro came out of her bedroom with both hands full of stuffing. They'd slashed her bed. He tossed the handfuls, and the stuffing scattered in clumps over Judith and the sofa. She pulled her robe closed.

"We've been watching you," he said, sneering.

Judith didn't say anything. The other dinosaurs came out and stood gathered there in front of her.

"We watch everyone," the dinosaur said after a moment, as though he'd decided he didn't want her to feel special after all.

"On this street?" said Judith. She wasn't sure she understood what he meant.

"We've never been here before. You'd know if we'd been here, believe me." The other dinosaurs laughed. One of them was poking at the sleepy man, checking his pockets and under the cushions of his chair.

"What did you see?" she asked him.

"You live like robots," he said. "Don't ask me any more questions."

One of the dinosaurs stepped up and pulled her hair and poked her gently in the eye. "Sorry," he said. Judith covered her eye with her hand. Another of the dinosaurs tuned the television to a station playing music, and turned the volume up so loud that the throb of the bass line was like an elephant's footsteps muffled in static.

"Hold her," said the dinosaur with the Afro. The girl on the sofa and the boy who'd poked Judith took her arms now and pinned her back against the cushions.

"What are you doing?" said Judith, frightened.

"Quiet." The one giving the orders pulled a roll of duct tape from his jacket. Judith thought: $12.99. He ripped a short patch of tape from the roll and pasted it across her mouth and, inadvertently, her nose. She could breathe through only one nostril. Suddenly all of her attention was devoted to the need to continue breathing.

The leader pulled open her robe and tore away her panties. They were old and ripped easily. He hurled the rent garment at the sleepy man, and it spread like a butterfly across his stomach and the arm of his chair. "Wake him up," said the leader. "Make him watch."

The sleepy man's head was to one side, his jaw slack. His right arm was still curled up beside his shoulder where it had held the cardboard tube. Judith wondered if they could sense the peacefulness that came from him. She saw in the corner of her vision that someone had knocked over the cactus, and it lay beside its pot in a sprawl of pebbles and dirt. She tried to struggle, but her arms were pinned back.

"Wake him up," said the leader again. He unfastened his belt and knelt between Judith's legs on the sofa. He didn't have an erection.

Judith tried to say, "He's asleep" but couldn't make a sound, and the effort drained her of air, so she had to focus on breathing again. Her entire head felt hot with blood, and her body felt cold and numb. The dinosaur's hand was on her chest, pressing her down as she tried to breathe. She imagined that her head was bright red and her body white and empty, sagging like the deflated growths of the cactus. She couldn't feel her body, just her bright hot head and the burning hand of the dinosaur against her chest.

"Wake him."

She saw that one of the dinosaurs, the eye poker, was slapping at the sleepy man now. Another was behind him, lifting the back of his chair, then jolting it down on the floor. She could barely hear the sounds over the noise of the television.

"Fuck, man."

"Is he dead?"

"Dead to the world."

He's only sleeping, thought Judith.

The leader made a disgusted sound and awkwardly got himself free of the sofa and the tangle of Judith's legs and robe. Judith felt his handprint fade from her chest. He went to the sleepy man and lifted his right eyelid, carefully, like a doctor. The other dinosaurs all watched. Then he buckled his belt and buttoned his pants. The television still blared, but it was the only sound. The girl released Judith's arm. Judith tugged the duct tape away from her nose. One of the dinosaurs that had been trying to wake the sleepy man was in the kitchen now, eating something. Another was in the bathroom, brushing her teeth with Judith's toothbrush. Judith pulled her robe closed.

The leader picked up the mailing tube and broke it easily over his knee. The halves didn't separate, but remained bound by a flexible curl of cardboard. The dinosaur who'd been in the kitchen emerged, chewing, and holding a big piece of bread. The leader slapped it out of his hand, and it landed on the sleepy man's lap, with the panties.

"Let's get out of here," he said.

"Can I take a shower?" said the tooth-brushing one from the bathroom.

Judith tore the patch of tape clear of her mouth. "It's okay," she said.

"Shut up," said the leader, pointing at her, but his heart definitely wasn't in it.

Judith cleaned up the mess and put everything that wasn't broken back in its place. She repotted the cactus, which didn't seem any the worse for wear, and put it on the kitchen windowsill where it had been before. Let the new growth take care of itself one way or the other, she thought. She didn't really need a bigger cactus.

Then she moved him from upright in the chair to supine on the sofa. She realized now how much better that was, how much less pretentious. She considered putting him out on the porch, but that seemed a little extreme. What happened wasn't his fault. The television went back into the closet; she didn't know who she was fooling with that one. She missed falling asleep to the sound of his breathing anyway.

At work the next morning she was alone in the office, wondering what had happened to Tom and Eva, and whether she would always be alone here now, when she thought to check a calendar and discovered it was Saturday. She wasn't supposed to be at work.

The militia came the following day. It had been raining through the night, and the air smelled washed. The sky was gray. They massed on her porch, admiral, lieutenant, sergeant, general, and others. They all wore baseball caps or hunting hats. Quick's son was along, carrying a pair of sagging duffel bags. Perhaps he'd been deputized, Judith thought. If that was the word for it. They knocked on her door, and when she came out, it was the admiral who addressed her. He carried a walking stick, and he gestured with the end of it.

"They raped you, didn't they?" he said.

"Not really," she said.

"Brave girl," said the admiral, shaking his head. Then he raised his stick and turned to the others. "They must be stopped," he declared.

"I don't think they're around," Judith said. "They went away."

"We'll find them," said the admiral.

"They can feel us breathing down their necks," said the sergeant, chuckling.

Judith had heard of this, of militias going mobile all of a sudden.

"We've come for Danny-boy," said the lieutenant. There was a note of sympathy in her voice, but Judith couldn't read her eyes, which were shaded with a green acetate insert behind her glasses.

"He's asleep," said Judith.

"R and R is over," said the sergeant.

"Besides, his mission's accomplished," said the admiral. "This position's no longer useful—it's *behind* us."

How did you know it was in front of you before? Judith wondered. But the sergeant and Quick's son were already past her and inside. They went to the sofa and took him by his arms, the sergeant saying, "Now is the time for all good men—"

John, Judith's former husband, stood a little behind the others, on the porch steps. The younger woman in the overalls stood with him. Judith looked at him. Suppressing a smile, he held out his hands and said, "It's true, Judith. A good scout has to stay ahead."

"I don't think he came here to scout," she said.

The sergeant and Quick's son had him up and walking, sort of. His head was drooped forward, and Judith could see that if they let go, he'd crumple. Yet he was planting one foot after another, moving forward. She felt a little proud, oddly enough. They got him through the door and across the porch, where John and the younger woman helped him down the steps and held him while Quick's son retook his duffel bags. No one but Quick's son had to carry any luggage, which testified to his low status within the militia. If he could even be said to be a part of it, Judith corrected. The sleepy man might only be a scout, but he was obviously crucial to them.

The admiral poked the end of his walking stick at the mat in front of her door. "What's this?"

The sergeant turned his head. "It says welcome," he said.

"That's hardly advisable," said the admiral.

The sergeant lifted the mat. "Might make a heck of a chest protector," he said, sizing it across his stomach. "May I?"

"Go ahead," said Judith.

The sergeant tucked the edge of the mat into his belt, so it projected like a section of cone from his waist, terminating at chin level. "Hey hey!" he said, beaming.

"We're off, then," said the lieutenant, moving aside to let the admiral use the steps. She clasped Judith's hand in both of hers. "For everything, thanks." Judith nodded, and the lieutenant turned away.

John and the younger woman had walked the sleepy man out to the curb. The rest of the militia trickled across the yard and bunched around them. Several of them put a hand out to help support the sleepy man, and they began to advance along the pavement. The sleepy man looked conspicuous among them without a hat, Judith thought. She hoped they'd find him one.

She stood and watched them from the porch. Soon they were at the end of the block, just a little black knot headed into the mist. She couldn't make out the sleepy man, couldn't distinguish any of them. God help him, she thought, then corrected it to, God help *them*. But that wasn't right either. God *bless* them? God bless us all? Just before they were completely out of sight she narrowed it to a curt *God bless*, as though someone had only sneezed.